PERTH AND KINROSS COUNCIL
LEISURE & CULTURAL SERVICES
LIBRARIES & ARCHIVES DIVISION

This book is due for return on or before the last date indicated
on label. Renewals may be obtained on application.

A ROSE CALLED MOONLIGHT

*Other titles by Elizabeth Daith available from
Severn House Large Print*

The Bronze Madonna
Emma and the Leprechauns
Green Spaces
Water in the Desert

A ROSE CALLED MOONLIGHT

Elizabeth Daish

Severn House Large Print
London & New York

This first large print edition published in Great Britain 2003 by
SEVERN HOUSE LARGE PRINT BOOKS LTD of
9-15, High Street, Sutton, Surrey, SM1 1DF.
First world regular print edition published 2002 by
Severn House Publishers, London and New York.
This first large print edition published in the USA 2003 by
SEVERN HOUSE PUBLISHERS INC., of
595 Madison Avenue, New York, NY 10022.

British Library Cataloguing in Publication Data

Daish, Elizabeth
   A rose called Moonlight - Large print ed.
   1.   Inheritance and succession - Fiction
   2.   Love stories
   3.   Large type books
   I.   Title
   823.9'14 [F]

ISBN 0-7278-7318-0

Printed and bound in Great Britain by
MPG Books Ltd, Bodmin, Cornwall.

For Jean and in memory of Arthur who found the rose called Moonlight

One

She had never been alone in the long gallery and it seemed even more unfamiliar in darkness than it did by daylight, but Charmian tried to stifle her fears and moved softly, listening.

The long windows were flooded with moonlight and the pillars of the balustrade cast long shadows which fell blackly across the hallway like iron bars.

She glanced back at the silent rooms and wondered if Mr Vaughn had heard it. If only she had his strength and the reassurance of his presence, she wished, but she was all alone.

She shuddered, the memory of her dream still with her. It had been so vivid that she wondered if it had only been a dream. She paused, looking back to the bend in the gallery where Deborah, her maid, still snored in the bedroom next to her young mistress's room, and she wished with all her heart that she was back under the safety of her canopied bed.

Should she awaken Deborah and tell her of her dream? Of the raised voices she had heard in the library? Men's voices cursing, and those other sounds: of steel on steel and shuffling feet on the parquet floor, laboured breathing and then silence?

She had come to the gallery to crouch behind the bars and to listen while she gazed down into the void of the moonlit hall. She half turned to go back, then held her breath. What was it? It sounded as if a shutter were swinging against a window in the library. There was a chink of light, a bright wedge shape in the doorway that changed as if candles flickered in a draught, but no sound now.

She frowned. The servants of the large house were well trained and would never leave lamps or candles lit after the family had gone to bed. It was possible that someone had forgotten to douse the lamps, but it was more likely that her father, Lord Altone, reluctant to leave his beloved books, might have sent Dermot to bed and been responsible himself for the oversight. Could there be nothing as simple as a light in the library to frighten a young girl?

But Charmian shivered in the warm June night, until a furry body moved against her arm and a comforting purring presence brought her to her senses. The cat sleekly moved around her in a half circle, pushing his nose into her hand. 'Kavanagh,' she whispered. 'Did you have bad dreams, too?' The cat stalked off down the stairs, but paused on the lower landing as if to make sure she followed him. He mewed plaintively. 'Are you thirsty?' asked Charmian, and smiled, forgetting her fear and her silly imaginings in this house that she had yet to call her true home.

'Come my pretty, we will find you milk,' she said. It was quite an adventure, being up in the middle of the night while the whole household of Hornbeam Manor slept and there was no fussy old Debby to tell her she must not waste good cream on a cat, even if he was Charmian's most precious memory of her old home in Wales.

She stole down softly and paused on the third stair from the bottom, which creaked badly. She listened again but nobody stirred in the dark upstairs rooms and Kavanagh mewed again, making for the chink of yellow light in the library doorway. She followed, curiosity overcoming her apprehension. Even if someone had been in there, he was gone now or it could not be so quiet. Kavanagh slipped into the room and arched his back. He spat at the thing he saw lying on the floor and jumped on to the study table.

A vase of full-blown roses went flying and water dripped down on to the bloodstain on the Aubusson rug, causing the crimson pool to spread, and a shower of yellow rose petals dropped softly down on to the face of the man who lay dead on the floor.

Charmian didn't see the the cat jump, but when she came in, she saw the spreading stain and the drift of yellow petals. She screamed and screamed and Deborah hurried down as fast as her short legs could carry her, clutching a woollen wrapper close to her plump body. She found her young mistress unconscious in a pathetic heap inside the door.

'What has happened, my love? Speak to me.' Deborah sat down and patted the ashen cheeks, and from the hall came hurrying footsteps and Dermot Turnville stood in the doorway. Deborah looked up. 'Oh Dermot, what has happened?' she

10

whispered.

'Murder,' he said, as he took his hand off the bloodstained shirt and the stillness where the pulse of life should have been beating. 'Murder, and it's the master who's dead.' He bent again to close the eyes of Peter, Lord Altone, head of the house, rich landowner and Charmian's father.

Other figures appeared in the moonlit hall. Prudence, the comely housekeeper and wife of Dermot, who with him made a pair of loyal and hardworking servants, who had loved the family so well that they had come with Lord Altone to Hornbeam Manor, long miles from their home on the Altone estates in Wales. They had left home and friends to stay with Charmian, so that his Lordship's new wife could enjoy the divertimentos that the elegant city of Bath had to offer, and where she could take her place in the fashionable society that she craved.

Prudence covered her face with her hands and sobbed, and Dermot moved towards her protectively. 'It's a sorry night's work,' he said.

'Who could do such a terrible thing?' wailed Prudence. 'Who would want to harm Lord Altone, the kindest man who ever

11

drew breath?'

The swirl of a silk peignoir made her look up. Helen, Lady Altone paused on the lower landing to look down on the assembly of family and servants. She smiled, but no warmth lit the clear blue eyes.

'My Lady,' whispered Deborah.

'Such noise! Who is responsible for making this fuss in the small hours? May I not have my slumber? You, girl ... Deborah, stop snivelling and tell me what's amiss.' She looked contemptuously at the shaking form of the woman who was bending over Charmian, then turned to Prudence who was trying to comfort Deborah. 'Have you too lost your tongue?' The ring of faces stared up at her as she walked slowly down to the hall. 'Come now, tell me,' she said with growing impatience. 'What is amiss?'

She saw the sorrow in Dermot's steady eyes, the noisy grief of Deborah and the still despair of the other servants and her hand clutched the front of her fragile garment as if it offered some protection from the doom-laden air.

She turned to the young man who was among the last to arrive. The shock and horror on his face was more positive a re-action, and she sensed that he would be of more use than the others. He was speaking to Dermot in a low voice by the door of the library.

'What is it, man?' he murmered anxiously.

'It's the master, sir. It's murder, Mr Vaughn.'

'My husband?' The voice of Lady Altone was sharp with alarm and Jack Vaughn glanced up at the graceful and beautiful woman who was now a widow for the second time. He took a step towards her, his brown eyes alight with compassion. His whole bearing showed all the signs of good breeding and the natural authority seldom found in poorly endowed younger sons and even less likely in the manners of paid librarians. Such was his position in life, but after only three months in the service of the earl, he had made a niche for himself in the great house and commanded the respect of all the household.

'Lord Altone is dead, My Lady.' He started forward. 'Look to her Ladyship, Mr Jaspern. She swoons,' he called to the man who had appeared behind his sister on the stairs.

Lady Altone pushed her brother away impatiently, declaring herself in complete control and telling him sharply not to fuss. She walked towards the library and the

13

servants drew back in silence as she looked down into the face of her dead husband. She was silent and pale; almost as pale as the face of the fainting girl.

Jack Vaughn bent over the girl and felt her wrist. 'She is recovering,' he said. He glanced at Deborah. 'Did she see anything of this? Does she know who killed her father? We must take her away so that it will not add to her distress if she wakes and sees him again.' He picked up the limp girl in his arms and turned to the stairs. 'Come Deborah, you must see your mistress into bed. I will carry her to her room.'

He felt her head sink deeper into his broad shoulder and she stirred in his arms. It was a movement that inspired in him an unfamiliar protective response and he was strangely moved that she should trust him, even in her sleep. He climbed the stairs slowly with Deborah bustling ahead to make sure the bed was neatly arranged to receive the precious burden.

Charmian sighed and her eyelids fluttered. He marvelled at the white skin brushed by the sweeping dark eyelashes. The scent of lavender came from her nightdress, and through the fine cambric and lace, he could feel her heart beating.

Almost without knowing what he did, he lightly kissed the closed eyes. Charmian smiled and put a hand round his neck, and from unconsciousness, she slipped into a deep and natural sleep, made safe by the strong arms and comforted by the light kisses.

He laid her on the bed with reluctance and Deborah hurriedly pulled down the long nightdress to cover the bare and trim ankles. She pulled the coverlet high under the girl's chin and breathed a sigh of relief. What would the master think if she failed in her duty and allowed young men to gaze on his daughter's sleeping form when it was so lightly clad?

Jack Vaughn stood motionless, looking down at the rounded cheeks, the long soft auburn hair clouding the white pillow and the pale skin. 'It is the sleeping beauty herself,' he whispered.

Deborah coughed. 'Thank you kindly, sir. I can manage now,' she said firmly. 'The child is asleep, the pretty innocent. She will need all the rest she can have, poor lamb.' She fussed about, tidying the the cluttered dressing table and putting the discarded slippers neatly together at the side of the bed.

'A child?' Jack Vaughn shook his head. She might be only seventeen, and have been sheltered in her upbringing in Wales, but the slender waist and gently swelling bosom he had clasped to his heart as he carried her to bed belonged to no child. For the first time since his arrival at the manor, with the preoccupation of his work, he saw Charmian for what she was: a budding beauty, very nearly a woman; a half-opened rose.

He paused on the turn from the gallery before descending the stairs, unwilling to relinquish the memory of the sweet moment when Charmian had twined her hand into the thick hair at the back of his neck. He braced his shoulders. This was no time to think of anything but the fact that his employer was dead. There were more important matters to attend to than the swooning fit of an immature girl.

He was confused. He descended the stairs with his head bowed under the many questions needing answers. Who had killed Lord Altone and what would happen at Hornbeam Manor now that tragedy had struck? What indeed would *he* do now that there was no enthusiastic patron to employ him to care for his books? He had begun a detailed catalogue of all the books in the library.

Would he now be sent away before it was done? Other employers would be easy to find, through the influence of his brother who had inherited the title and most of the wealth of Jack Vaughn's family. It might be teaching in a boys' school, or in the capacity of secretary. But it would be far away from the family who had treated him as one of themselves for the three short and happy months he had known them.

There was a dark patch on the stair below him. It was odd to see fresh mud on the polished wood. He stooped to touch it. The mud was soft, but in one piece as if moulded, and the shape it held was one which could fit the space between the high heel and the curve of the sole of a gentleman's riding boot.

Jack Vaughn joined the group in the hall. Lady Altone was sitting on the couch in a nook by the door and her brother, Melville Jaspern, was by her side. They regarded Jack Vaughn coldly. 'How is my stepdaughter?' asked Lady Altone. 'I thank you for your services, sir, but I do not approve of young men in a lady's bedchamber.' She raised an imperious hand as he tried to speak. 'You are very kind, Mr Vaughn, but there will be no call for you to visit her again in her room.

The family will look after her, and there are enough idle servants here to run to her bidding. I suggest you concentrate on the task for which you are employed, the catalogue in the library.'

'And would you have me leave the child on the cold floor when her bed was so near? Would you have wished her to wake to further shock, My Lady?' His concern gave him self-assurance and he stood tall, regarding her with pain in his eyes.

The tension left Lady Altone's face and she smiled, sensing his manhood and strength and undoubted good looks. She smiled an apology. 'Forgive me, Mr Vaughn. I am too careful of my dear stepdaughter. She is, as you say, a child and must be protected from all such matters. However, it will be the duty of my brother, his very special duty, to entertain Charmian and erase from her mind all that has happened tonight. He must help us both to recover from this tragedy.' Her delicate fingers fluttered over her brow. 'We are all tired, so very tired, and there is nothing we can do tonight. I suggest we return to our rooms to rest. We shall need strength to compose ourselves for the Runners who come from London tomorrow to ask questions. The coach

18

has left to bring them, but it will take time.'

'And his Lordship?'

'My ... my late husband is still in the library. Dermot is with him and will do what is necessary.'

Jack Vaughn took the lovely hand extended to him and helped Lady Altone to her feet. She clung to him for a moment, and he knew why the rakes of Bath toasted her and the dandies of London called her the Lily of Altone. She was very beautiful in a crystal-clear, fair-haired way. The crystal glinted with bright light but was not soft or restful. Her hand was cool and shapely, but it lacked the softness of the fingers which had curled like a baby's in the nape of his neck when he had carried Charmian to her room.

He glanced at Lady Altone's face in the lamplight. The blue eyes were tired and he felt guilty that his first impression had been that she was hard and cold. Under that magnificent self-discipline, there must be a wealth of feeling, a well of emotion to which she would surrender only in the privacy of her rooms. He couldn't help but admire the proud and regal bearing in her hour of great personal loss. 'Your servant, ma'am,' he said fervently, and a shaft of warmth lit her face and for the first time that night reached her eyes.

'May I depend on you, Jack? I need your loyalty and friendship.' She pressed his hand between her own and he felt a silver cord of her beauty binding him to her service.

'Whenever you need me,' he said simply, and Lady Altone walked away to the stairs, followed by Prudence, whose eyes were still swollen from weeping but who had recovered enough to prepare a tisane of camomile for her mistress before helping her to bed.

Melville Jaspern sat down again and absent-mindedly felt in the pockets of his dressing robe for a snuff box. He seemed surprised to find himself dressed for bed and made a movement to open the gown as if to search other pockets beneath the robe. Instead, he hastily clutched it closer and glanced anxiously at Mr Vaughn, but the young man's attention was lifted towards the gallery along which Lady Altone walked, a vision of ethereal paleness, of fair hair, blue gown and a cascade of ecru lace.

Melville murmured a goodnight and followed her up the stairs, and Jack Vaughn saw that he wore riding boots of fine leather with high heels under the voluminous robe. Melville Jaspern riding? At four in the morning? He did not think it necessary to advertise the fact, but instead Jack paced the hall, recalling the moment when Lady Altone had seemed to sway on the stairs and nearly swoon. Melville had been standing close by her, but had said nothing. He gave the impression that he too was recovering from shock, and he had obviously been under a considerable strain as he seemed breathless. Had he run to his sister's side or had he been riding hard? He had appeared long after the screams had alerted the servants, and if he had been awake he should have heard the commotion earlier and been the first, not one of the last, on the scene. What man slept in riding boots?

Jack Vaughn stifled a yawn of utter weariness as emotion and fatigue took their toll. He climbed the stairs and paused by Charmian's door. 'Goodnight, sweet child,' he said. She was a child compared to the brilliance of Lady Helen.

In the library, Dermot lit a lamp by the trestle table that held the mortal remains of his master. He began to clean the stain from the carpet, but first brushed up the limp rose petals from the floor. His hand touched something cold and round that gleamed in the lamplight. He put it in his pocket, together with a scrap of Brussels lace he found, cut or torn from the wrist frill of a very expensive shirt that would only be worn by a gentleman of means. 'One day, My Lord, I'll avenge this foul killing,' he swore. 'I'll find him, see if I don't.' He spread a warm rug on the settle and trimmed the fire in the wide hearth, doused the lamp and said his prayers, then kept vigil for his master until weariness overcame him and, like the rest of the household, he fell asleep.

The silence was complete, but as the fire died, Dermot awoke and groped for the rug that had slipped to the floor. He listened and knew that the silence held a small sound, a movement outside the unlatched door.

He lay still, feigning sleep as soft footsteps stopped by the door and the hinges creaked as the heavy door swung open enough to admit a dark figure, muffled up in a long surcoat that hid him up to his tricorne hat. He stooped low, searching the floor at the spot where Dermot had cleaned the carpet. Dermot saw only the outline and nothing of the man's face, but he did see hands moving feverishly over the floor and heard the muted curses as they touched the cold, wet carpet. This was no member of the household, but a stranger, in a dark surcoat such as coachmen wore.

Dermot moved and flung back the rug, calling, 'Who is there?'

The stranger backed towards the door and the full length of the room was between them. Dermot almost fell in the cumbrous folds of the rug and the man seized the key from the inside lock and slipped out, locking the door behind him.

Dermot wrestled with the handle and shouted, but he knew that no one would hear him either through the thick oak door or the heavy window curtains and shuttered windows.

He heard a door slam once he managed to open a shutter, and tried to look out, but it was impossible to say from whence the sound came. He fingered the silver button in his pocket and wondered who had thought it important enough to seek, at the risk of discovery. He shrugged and settled down to sleep again until dawn, when Prudence came in with ale to call him and to release him.

Two

'You must eat, my love. It's no use starving yourself when all your grieving can never bring him back.' Deborah sat by the bed and tried to persuade her young mistress to eat some of the fresh junket and cream she had brought in a silver dish, but Charmian refused to look at it. Debbie clucked helplessly and put the dish away.

'If I could but remember, Deb. I *must* remember, but each time I am close to knowing who was with my father, a blanket falls over my mind. If the events were true and no dream, then I must know the voice I heard. There must be something I can recall, but how can I bring it back?' She flung herself on the bed and buried her face in the pillow while the woman stroked her tousled hair.

'Help me to think, Debbie. It must be

24

someone who knows the house. It is someone known to my father and possibly someone I have met.'

Deborah shrugged wearily and tried to comfort her, murmuring meaningless words that she used whenever Charmian needed consoling, since the three-month-old baby girl had come into the woman's care when the first Lady Altone died of milk fever.

Debbie glanced at the case clock in the corner and stood up. In the voice of authority, which was a privilege of long service, she said, 'Come now, you will do no good straining to remember. It will come to you when you least expect it. The doctor says so. It's time to dry your eyes, my lamb.' She went to the dressing table and picked up a hairbrush. 'You must let me dress your hair. What will her Ladyship say if you are not downstairs again when she summons you? She asked to see you yesterday after the Runners left the manor.' Deb's cheeks flushed with indignation. 'Such rough, uncouth fellows, sitting on his Lordship's velvet couch, with dirty boots on the Aubusson carpet. I soon told them to show a little respect! And what good were they? They upset the whole household by asking a great many foolish questions of all the wrong people, if you ask me,' she added darkly.

'What do you mean?' Charmian thought back to the scene in the withdrawing room, much of which she had thankfully missed as it was thought to be of too much of an ordeal for one so young after her terrible discovery, when she found her father dead in the library.

She recalled with gratitude the friendly face and strong arm of Mr Vaughn, who had helped her to a seat and then stayed with her while the few questions were asked and had then firmly said that she had answered enough questions and must rest. She had leaned on his arm and been safe. He was so strong and manly and a real friend, who could, she felt sure, be very formidable if crossed, and his demeanour had impressed the Bow Street Runners, even though he was was of no important rank, as a second son, with no hope of inheriting more than a pittance from his family estates.

She sighed. 'Mr Vaughn was kind. I was not there for more than a few minutes. He escorted me back to my room and asked Pru to bring me hot chocolate.'

'And when he was out of the room, the Runners got it into their thick skulls that the murderer must have known the master well and hinted that Mr Vaughn might have had something to do with it.' Deborah sniffed. 'They didn't like being told off by a man who is only a librarian, and they gave him a bad time when he returned to the room. They said that as he was new to the household he would have no fixed loyalties and must be after something of value.

'I was serving them drink and couldn't keep a still tongue. "Go and look elsewhere," I said. "Look in the hedgerows for some rascally footpad, or one of those highwaymen seen over the bridge of Avon last week. Look there, and you'll find your murderer, not in his Lordship's drawing room." They didn't like it,' she continued. '"Go and do your duty in some other place. Have you no stomach for such work?" I told them.' She flushed at the memory. 'Mr Vaughn stopped me and said that they were only doing their duty and must ask questions according to their lights.'

'Mr Vaughn? Why did they think ill of him, Deb?'

'It seems that he was one of the last to appear when you screamed. They said he could have gone out by the library window and back in through the door.'

'Who said that?'

'Mr Jaspern hinted as much and said that Mr Vaughn acted in a strange manner. I said that Mr Vaughn *cared* and showed that he cared, which was more than his high and-mightyness did. I told the Runners that Mr Jaspern had been out. He could have come in the back way as easily. I know he was out because Dermot had to clean his riding boots as they were covered with mud.' She shrugged. 'Her Ladyship told me to hold my tongue or she'd have me dismissed.'

'What did the Runners say?'

'They sat there, toasting their toes and drinking wine that Mr Jaspern sent for them to drink.' Deborah was almost incoherent with anger. 'They touched their hats and drank his health as if *he* was the lord of the manor. They were told that Dermot knew the truth and that Mr Jaspern had already explained why he was riding at night, after a late session at the gaming tables in Bath. He told them he had begun to undress when his sister, her Ladyship, came to his room asking if he'd heard a noise.'

Charmian slipped out of bed and allowed Debbie to brush her hair, then took the brush from her and coiled her hair high on her head like a bright coronet. She held it so, looking at her reflection in the heavy mirror that hung from a gilt frame above the dressing chest.

Debbie took the brush again and firmly arranged the hair in a style more suitable for a young girl who had not, as yet, been presented at court or come of age.

'Time enough for you to put up your hair, my child,' she said, but her heart was sad and she was filled with strange feelings of dread. Soon, too soon, her young charge would be a lovely young woman, with no father or mother to care for her and to see that she made a fitting choice for a happy marriage. What might become of her? She was blossoming and becoming aware of all that life could offer ... but not of what life could take away.

It was one thing for Mr Vaughn to look at Charmian with respectful admiration, but what of the others who flocked round the newly-widowed Lady Altone? Would Lady Altone's friends show the same respect due to the daughter of one of Britain's oldest families?

Debbie dressed her simply, and as Charmian went down to the drawing room, Debbie thought of Lady Altone and her handsome fair-haired brother, Melville Jaspern, who seemed to have nothing better to do than to live at Hornbeam Manor as a permanent guest, frequenting the gaming tables and soirées in the Assembly Rooms in Bath.

Debbie watched Charmian go down the sweeping stairway and twisted her fingers in her apron, feeling helpless. She had seen that look of cool appraisal that Melville Jaspern gave to the child, but she was powerless to prevent them meeting. It was useless to put off the inevitable, although Pru had been obliged to tap several times on the bedroom door to make Debbie send her mistress down to meet with Lady Altone.

Prudence followed Charmian down the stairs, relieved to see that she had recovered enough to meet Lady Altone, who was in no mood to be thwarted and was growing impatient. She tweaked Charmian's long sash into flat obedience, as if sending a child off to a tea party, and opened the door for Charmian to enter the room.

But this was no birthday party for an indulged child. The lawyers stood in dark suits more suitable for church than for the bright and elegant room of gold and chartreuse silks and velvet. Mr Vaughn smiled at her and Charmian felt her tension lessen, but he quickly turned away to resume the explanation of a document that the lawyer was studying. He was patient, and when Lady Helen asked questions in a cold voice, he was careful to tell her simply what she was required to understand. His warmth seemed to soften the woman in the high-backed gilt chair, and as Prudence left the room, she wondered if Charmian would have any friends left at Hornbeam Manor apart from her and Debbie and Dermot, if Mr Vaughn fell under the spell of the lovely widow.

Who could resist her if she showed the side of her nature that hinted at fragility and allure? What man could resist her if she wanted him?

If only Lord Altone had remained in Wales among the beautiful rolling hills and remote valleys, where every last villager loved and respected his name and cared about his family. She thought of the sons of local Welsh landowners and gentry, dark-haired and stout-limbed, with wealth and lands and sense enough to make any of them a suitable match for Charmian. They had something that Prudence missed in the faces of the new friends who flocked to Lady Altone's shrine: they had devotion and honesty.

The young men of Wales might be blunt and almost rude in their honesty, but they were loving and true to any they called friend, and with any of these men, Charmian could have love, security and laughter.

She left the room, bobbing and smoothing her apron as Lady Altone waved her away, impatient for the business of the day. Melville Jaspern smiled at Charmian, his face warm with admiration as he left his seat to take the girl's hand in his before the assembled company. He drew her closer, and kissed her cheek lightly. 'My privilege,' he said softly. 'I am your uncle by marriage, am I not? I have the right.' His lazy smile froze as Charmian flushed and drew away. It was not the blush of a girl flattered by a handsome man. She was annoyed, as if he presumed too much upon their relationship.

The lawyer, Mr Lanyon, grunted and his mouth lost some of the hard lines it normally assumed when he was on official business. The girl wasn't ready for young bucks and their flattery. She had spirit and natural common sense, and he hoped she might be able to hold her own with the handsome dilettante and his beautiful sister, who seemed to dominate the room as if they owned it all to the exclusion of any blood relative.

'La, child, and are you well again?' asked Lady Altone. 'My poor brother has been quite distracted and I have been hard put to keep him from invading your room to see for himself that you are recovered.'

'Thank you, ma'am, but I am well,' said Charmian with a proud lift to her head. She forbore to look at Melville but had a dangerous glint in her eyes. To Mr Vaughn, the pinkness of the soft cheeks meant that she was aware of the male flattery and he experienced a curious sadness and something he couldn't recognize beyond a certain annoyance.

He looked at the man who still sat by Charmian's side, and he had to admit that as far as appearances went, Melville would seem the perfect match for the lovely but immature girl. The well cut velvet jacket with bronze buttons and the dandified cravat, worn in an attempt to copy the fashionable image set by the beaux of Bath, were worn with confidence and style. His noble bearing and the help of a good tailor showed as he sat, elegantly turning one silk clad leg to show the gleaming buckle of his shoe and the lustre of the silk hose.

Jack Vaughn felt suddenly poor in his fustian jacket. He was poor in dress, in financial hopes and spirit, and his future prospects rested on the ability to attract a patron, further work with books or in marrying someone with land who would enjoy being linked by marriage to the title now borne by his brother.

Why think of that now? Two days ago he had been content and thought of nothing but the pleasant hours spent in the lovely house with people who had welcomed him so readily. An accident of birth and his brother took everything apart from a house on the estate and a small stipend. What could he offer to any woman of rank?

He started, looking down at the bejewelled hand on his wrist.

'What ails you, Mr Vaughn? Have I lost your attention?' Lady Altone smiled a gentle but reproving smile and he felt a thread of fire coming from her fingers; the pull of her cool beauty as dazzling as the flash of the diamonds on her fingers. It was the beauty of sunlight on ice.

Charmian saw the admiration in his eyes and the fleeting triumph on the woman's face and knew that she was excluded.

'Well now,' said her Ladyship, who seemed

34

to have recovered her good humour in spite of the fact that her husband was so newly dead. 'The lawyers are very tedious, my dear, but Mr Vaughn is being very patient and efficient and has all the documents in order. He is dealing with such a big estate but is making sure that even a simple woman can understand.' She gave him a sweet smile. 'These gentlemen have their duties to perform as they see fitting, so now that you are with us at last, dear child, we can begin this dreary business.' She nodded imperiously to the lawyer. 'Pray proceed, sir, and tell my stepdaughter what she may ... what *we* may expect.'

She reclined gracefully with a faint smile on her lips and Melville went to lean against the back of her chaise, looking bored as if estates and vulgar money were beneath his interest. Mr Vaughn bowed and left the room while the details of the last will and testament of the noble Lord were read by Mr Lanyon in a clear, dry voice that gave away nothing of his private feelings.

As he read, Lady Altone grew tense, and as the details of the will were revealed, her hands twisted in the soft silk of her robe and tore at the lace trimming. Her fingers clenched and unclenched on her lap and she pulled at the heavy rings in an agony of rage and frustration, but her face remained beautiful and icily calm.

Charmian noticed the hands, as did Mr Dark, the clerk who had come with Mr Lanyon. Melville put a hand on the shoulder of the perfumed woman who had promised him so much, and he grew apprehensive.

'So,' said the lawyer after an hour of droning. 'That is the gist of the details of the property and of Lord Altone's intentions. Lady Charmian, you will receive a generous allowance to keep up the entire estate until you are twenty-one and you will keep the management as before until that date, when you will receive full control over all your properties.' He coughed. 'I have two duties here today. The melancholy task of offering my sincere condolences to you, my dear. I knew, liked and respected your father and with your permission will do all in my power to safeguard the inheritance he left for you.' He coughed again in an embarrassed manner. 'The other duty, a more pleasant one, or it would be in happier circumstances, is to congratulate you, which I do most heartily, my dear. You are now a very wealthy young woman.'

He rustled the papers on the desk. 'May I

offer some advice as a friend of your father's and I hope as your friend too?' His manner dropped its dry gruffness and his eyes were gentle. 'Be careful. Be very careful. With this wealth, you will find half the fortune hunters in London and Bath, and possibly in Europe, after you. You have wealth and beauty and I hope the brains that will help you to choose wisely and be happy, but promise me that you will make no major decisions before consulting me. Your father appointed me your trustee and I intend to take that duty seriously. It will be a great pleasure and—' he glanced at Lady Altone — 'I shall watch over you and pray for your protection at all times, my dear.'

He went to the silent girl and took her hand. She looked up at him with a surge of new confidence and clung to his arm in an effort to delay his departure. She knew he was a rock of safety and she needed his protection but couldn't think why. He was a link to help her into a new life. 'You will stay a while?' she begged. 'You must stay at least until after luncheon,' she added weakly.

'With pleasure.' He smiled. 'It will be a real pleasure, but first we must walk a little in the garden and we shall talk.' He offered her his arm and led her to the open glass doors leading to the sunken garden and the rose terrace.

'Are you not forgetting?' They turned at the door. 'You are mistress here now,' said the icy voice. 'You must give the orders now that your father has seen fit to reduce me to pauperdom, a widow with no substance, a mere dependent on a small allotment. I have no authority here nor wish to assume such authority.' The controlled fury in the chilling voice made Charmian shiver and cling to the lawyer's arm tightly. The harsh voice continued relentlessly. 'You must take over the house, the accounts and the menus—'

Mr Lanyon cut across the fury. 'No, ma'am! You must not kick against your husband's wishes. Think carefully. He made generous provision for you and you bear his noble name, which gives you entrée into the bon ton of high society. As you must recall, he asked you to care for his daughter and to shelter her from the commitment of running a house until she is eighteen.'

Lady Altone tossed her head and stood up, thrusting the chaise longue back so that it slid upon the polished floor. 'A paid housekeeper!' she said and swept from the room, with Melville following her as if in a dream.

Mr Dark also left to find Jack Vaughn and to tell him the course of events.

'She is very vexed,' Charmian said.

'No need for you to be upset, my dear,' Mr Lanyon said. 'Now all my duty has been done, I beg your permission to speak freely. I have been a friend of this family for many years. I first saw you as a roguish infant in a bassinet.' Charmian hugged his arm. 'Well child, it's not my place to say this, but I will,' he said bluntly. 'Take care of all the handsome faces you'll see, and there'll be enough of them, you may be sure. Take care of not only the ones you'll meet when you come of age, but take care of those you meet closer to home. Fortune hunters come in many disguises and they can make themselves attractive to a lonely girl.'

They strolled between the yew hedges that were clipped in many shapes, and on to the rose garden where they paced the flat paths. 'But I am safe here, sir. There is no one here to fear. I have met so few people since we left Wales. There is only Mr Vaughn and Melville.' Her smile died as she saw his expression.

'I have said nothing. I seldom name names as it's too dangerous in my profession, but keep all parties in mind, and everyone you meet and have reason to believe might be fond of you for one reason or another. Now,' he said gently, 'there is one you can trust. Prudence is sound and I've talked to her, and Dermot, her husband. You can trust your life to him, and to your old maid, Deborah.'

'I know that I have their love,' she said.

'Prudence was saying that you tried to recall the voice that you thought you heard in a dream, or possibly reality, on that terrible night.'

'Yes, I try to hear it again until my head aches and then just as I think I have it, it is gone. I still have the idea that I know it and will know the voice if I hear it again.'

Mr Lanyon drew her into the shelter of a tall topiary hedge fashioned like a swan. 'I don't want to alarm you unduly, but facts are facts. Someone killed your father and he must be found. As yet the villain is free and he'll want to remain so or face the Kingsdown gibbet.'

Charmian stared, wide-eyed. 'I'd almost forgotten. I've been so full of tears for my father that I had almost forgotten that there is a man behind the voice.' She frowned. 'I was on the stairs and heard a noise. I must have been half-asleep.' She looked dreamily across a bed of roses. There they were, her father's favourite flowers, bushes he'd brought from Wales from the rose garden there. What were they? They were creamy yellow, pale with the coolness of lemons, and were called Moonlight.

'What is it, my dear? You are pale.' The lawyer looked round helplessly, wishing a female would appear.

'It's nothing. Something in my mind stirred. These roses were my father's favourite flowers and he had them in his library. He showed them to his guests only last month when they were still in bud.'

Footsteps came along the upper path. 'We haven't much time,' Mr Lanyon said urgently. 'I beg you to promise me that if you recall anything more about that night or hear the voice again, you will tell nobody until you have spoken to me. You must pretend that it is still a mystery to you.'

The footsteps came closer. 'Promise me or you may be in danger!'

'I promise,' Charmian said. 'I solemnly promise that I shall tell not a single soul, even Debbie, but will you come quickly if I send word? You *will* come here very often to see me? That must be your promise.'

'Make no mistake, I shall be a very

frequent visitor,' he said grimly.

'My dear sister has the vapours.' A cynical voice broke into their thoughts. 'She seems a trifle put about, and the vapours seem as good an excuse for a fit of the sulks as any I know.' Melville flipped the wide tail of his coat to one side and sat on a slender garden chair. 'You will excuse the liberty?' His face was now on a level with Charmian's as she sat on the rustic bench. 'I was out very late and I am tired.' He sighed. 'All for nought, it was an unprofitable night's work.'

'The gaming tables?' Mr Lanyon frowned. 'Take heed, my dear. Nothing good came of throwing hard-earned money away so lightly.'

Charmian saw that Melville was displeased as if he hoped that he'd have the sympathy of another man and not this tight-lipped disapproval.

'Come sir,' Melville said in a forced jovial tone, 'we are men of the world, are we not? You cannot deny that fortunes have been made at the tables?'

'We hear of such matters, but seldom of the ones that disappear at the throw of a dice.' The lawyer smiled. 'How glad I am that Miss Charmian cannot indulge in such activities without my consent.' He turned to her. 'Of course, my dear, if you wish to amuse yourself with a modest sum when you are eighteen, you will be free to do so, but I hope that by then, you will have learned of the folly that such amusements bring.'

Charmian nodded. 'My father disliked all gambling, sir. That's one of the reasons...' She blushed, recalling high voices when Lady Helen tried to explain away a debt brought from Bath in which she and her brother were equally involved.

'Exactly,' Mr Lanyon said dryly.

Melville laughed and seemed to dismiss the subject as of no importance. It was evident that the lawyer was too much of a dried old stick to have sympathy with the life and ambitions of a young and handsome rake. A small loan from him now seemed out of the question. His sister had been right. The sooner he set about ensnaring the young heiress, the sooner would their joint futures be secure. Without money, what was life in Bath or London or Brighton, should he catch the attention of the Prince Regent?

He leaned forward, his face full of concern. 'You look done-up, Charmian. It's unfair to make you think of money and documents so soon after your father's death. So much has happened and you've had no fun. You need cheering up and I am the man to do that. I suggest, my dear sir, a little Madeira before luncheon and a glass of sherry for Charmian to bring the roses back to her cheeks.'

Somehow, without noticing how it had been arranged, Charmian found her hand on Melville's arm as they walked back to the house, with Mr Lanyon following more slowly, full of misgivings so vague that in any other situation they would have had no place in his legal mind.

Three

'Do you really care for that?' Jack Vaughn stood by the long side table and smiled down at Charmian. She glanced across to where Melville was talking to Mr Dark, the lawyer's clerk and secretary. She smiled with a conspiratorial gleam in her eyes and handed the Venetian glass to the young librarian.

'I dislike it, Mr Vaughn, but it is sometimes easier to accept a glass and to leave it untouched than to make much of something unimportant.' She saw that he had no glass of his own. 'Pray accept this, Mr Vaughn,' she said with a mock curtsey. 'You are too late for Madeira, I believe, but the sherry is good.'

He too had noticed that Melville was drinking freely and the level of Madeira was low in the decanter.

He sipped the pale gold liquid, enjoying the freshness of the girl's face and her sudden glimmer of humour. She was as unspoiled as the bright flowers on the terrace outside, and his heart warmed with something akin to affectionate protectiveness. It came as a shock to know he felt such gladness in the fact that she had refused a gesture of giving from Melville Jaspern, even if it was a trivial offer of a glass of sherry.

'I believe that the lawyers have finished their business, Lady Charmian. I hope that now you will find time for more pleasing occupations?' Vaughn asked.

'Like gambling, sir?' she replied.

'Certainly not that. Whatever made you think I'd suggest such an occupation for a young girl?' His face darkened. Who had been filling her mind with such matters? 'I mean more fitting and bracing occupations, M'lady.'

His tone made her feel that they were generations apart and she blushed with resentment. He was her father's librarian and could be only six and twenty years of age, and certainly no older than Melville, who treated her with the flattery due to a young woman only a year away from

46

her eighteenth birthday and presentation at court.

'I have no wish to arrange flowers or to sew, sir,' she said stiffly.

'Nor should you. You may leave all that until you are in charge of your establishment. Young girls should play and ride and walk, go boating on the lake and also ... study!'

'You sound like my governess and I have no need of tutors now.' She drew herself up tall but he still towered above her. 'I read and visit and I shall soon have to prepare for London and the season.'

'So soon?' His dark eyes were sad. Her lips were trembling and she looked so young and vulnerable that he wanted to bend to kiss the gentle lips and to chase away anything that could harm her. He flushed slightly as he recalled the night when her father was killed. He had taken that liberty when his arms held her close as he carried her to her room. Quickly, he recovered his poise. 'But you will have time to ride. If I can offer my services as escort, I ride each morning, but always early.'

'Oh, yes!' Her eyes shone with the excitement of a child. 'And shall we gallop so fast that we can blow away all the dullness of this house?'

'You miss the hills of Wales?' He took her by the hand. 'I think we must go in to luncheon. I am invited and the lawyers are staying.'

Her hand rested on his arm and she found the contact comfortable and wondered if Mr Vaughn had sisters of whom he was fond, or was there a girl with whom he was in love? She looked up into his face and hoped that he would stay at Hornbeam Manor for a very long time.

Melville sat across the other side of the table and poured claret into a fine goblet, ignoring the polite duty of a gentleman to look after the guests to his right and left. He seemed morose, as well he might be, as he'd lost heavily at chemin de fer the previous night. His hopes, and the anticipation he'd felt when he thought of the fortune that his sister would have on the death of her husband, were now shattered. True, she would be comfortable and had enough for a woman to live in luxury, but it hardly amounted to a fortune that could be lavished on a deserving brother.

He wasted no thought for his dead brother-in-law, except to curse him for tying up the estates so firmly that nobody with itching fingers could touch the immense wealth involved. Everything was so difficult and there was no understanding left in the world! Mr Lanyon was not one to be deceived into giving away any of Charmian's trust to a man with no title and no money and no energy to engage in a profitable and worthwhile venture that entailed work.

Would he stake me in some form of business? he mused. One glance at the square chin and sombre businesslike eyebrows caused him to sigh. He'd be tedious and demand facts and figures, potential profit and loss. He wasn't the man for it. He looked across at the young librarian who sat with Lady Altone, further down the table. The lady had pointedly vacated her place as mistress of the household and taken a very lowly seat at the table, begging Mr Vaughn to sit with her and keep her company.

Her hand on his arm and her perfume in his nostrils, together with the air of fragility that said she was cast low by circumstances and conspiracy and needed the help of a strong man who suffered as she did under the protocol of the time, made Mr Vaughn give her his full attention, and Charmian found herself being led to the head of the table, with Mr Lanyon for company and the rural dean on her other side.

Lady Altone looked quietly resigned to her fate and Charmian blushed with embarrassment, but Vaughn attended to her Ladyship with devoted care and Melville wondered how deep that devotion could go. Jack Vaughn had no money and no title but was nobly bred. He had no hope of support other than through his own efforts, perhaps as secretary to a rich patron, or teaching unruly brats. Could he be bent to any advantage? Melville contemplated the idea while Jack Vaughn talked to Lady Altone, his eyes bright, his manner eager and his love of books evident as he told her of some rare books in the library collection that he had found while cataloguing.

'Are they valuable?' Helen asked with only half her attention, but she smiled sweetly as she would at any man as attractive as Jack Vaughn. Melville strained to hear what was being said.

'Books, did you say?' asked Mr Lanyon.

'I was compiling an inventory, sir, and I was hoping to have it completed soon,' Mr Vaughn said. He looked from Charmian to Mr Lanyon uncertainly. Now that his patron was dead, who would care for inventories and who would want to keep him in the employ of the manor?

'I'm glad you raised that point, Mr Vaughn.' The lawyer turned to Charmian. 'I hope you have no objections, my dear. I would like Mr Vaughn to remain here. In my opinion, you will be glad of his expertise for many months to come. The house and contents were bought with, in my opinion, such unnecessary haste, with no proper inspection of the value or otherwise, that there is much to be done.' He eyed Helen accusingly. 'I cannot help thinking that if Lord Altone had remained in Wales, he would be alive today.'

'La, sir, and would you have me rot in the country? Could a lady be expected to live in a place where it rains for most of the year and there are only cows and clodhoppers for company?'

The lawyer ignored her bewitching smile. 'I could suggest selling or renting this house on lease, Lady Charmian, as the house can hold no good memories for you.' He sensed Helen's alarm and smiled grimly. 'But,' he continued, with a sigh, 'all things grow up, more's the pity, and you will have to be presented at court next year. This address is as good as any for county circles.' He bent over his dish, a hint of humour on his lips.

'We shall have to find someone to take you in hand; someone who knows all about the taradiddles a young woman thinks she needs; someone who knows court etiquette.' He paused to drink some of the excellent claret and saw that Helen almost held her breath. 'Naturally there would be provision made for that. Whoever took on the task would deserve a very fair allowance, even a generous one for someone willing to give so much time and care for so long.' He sipped again. 'Let me think. We shall need someone prepared to bring you out, honourably, self-lessly and with a true sense of occasion. No menial person would do, but a lady of talent, taste and elegance.'

He seemed lost in thought. 'There will be no need to look far, sir.' Helen said. 'There is no need to bother Charmian's Welsh relatives with such trifles, unless you want her as inelegant as *les traineusses* in France, the jumped-up bourgeoisie, who can't manage a court train or stand upright and walk on highly polished floors.' She smiled at the girl with such warmth that Charmian wondered where the ice had gone and couldn't help but smile back.

'It would take all your time for several months,' Mr Lanyon said.

'My dear,' Helen said, 'if I promise Mr Lanyon to be very patient with you and make you work hard, may I make you ready for court?' Her coldness was gone and it was easy to see how Lord Altone became ensnared by the lovely woman, who he met and married in the space of four months.

He'd had four months of happiness and another four before she'd become bored and invited her friends to replace the warmth and humour of the Welsh families.

When they'd exchanged the Welsh hills for the sophistication of Bath, her friends had come to the house and it was then, Mr Lanyon recalled, that Lord Altone journeyed to Lincoln's Inn, white with rage at the latest invasion of his privacy, the extreme wanton extravagance of his wife and the presence of her brother who hung about the house like a parasite, eating and drinking and riding hard, staying out until all hours gambling and borrowing money from whosoever was fool enough to indulge him.

Mr Lanyon coughed. 'It would seem that you must be the obvious choice, ma'am, but in a codicil to the will, I am appointed sole executor and any expense must be sanctioned by me. If you find that situation unacceptable, please say so now, and I can then appoint another lady to whom I might not seem so unreasonable.'

Charmian saw the twinkle in the lawyer's eyes and Helen's fingers dig into the table linen. Dear man, she thought, You have the measure of the lady and she has the sense to know it.

'Of course, it shall be as you say,' Helen conceded graciously.

'Good! Now, Mr Vaughn.' Jack Vaughn tore his gaze away from Helen. 'I should be obliged if you would continue in the employ of the estates, answerable to me in all matters. I need a secretary and accountant to be here and also to visit the Welsh estates, seeing over all matters concerning the income thereof. Will you undertake this task, sir? To keep the books, to conserve Lady Charmian's interest beyond those of any other party should the need arise? I am convinced that you are an honest man.' His voice had returned to that of a dry, toneless lawyer's and sounded as if he expected the young man to swear an oath of fealty. 'Of course, your salary would reflect your preferment and be commensurate with your responsibilities,' he concluded.

'I shall be honoured, sir.' Jack Vaughn seemed stunned. He looked at Charmian and his eyes were steadfast. 'You may trust me implicitly, Lady Charmian,' he said. She blushed under the intent gaze, and with a shock he saw the woman she might become. She was no child even now, dressed in the pretty smock of pale pink cambric, with her hair caught back in a simple snood. Her eyes held a plea and his heart lurched with tenderness for her.

She dropped her gaze and thought how sweet his mouth was; not as full and handsome as Melville's, but stronger and more gentle.

'So be it,' said Mr Lanyon. 'Now, if you will excuse me, Lady Charmian, I must be on my way with my clerk, but first I would like to be alone with Mr Vaughn in the library.'

He stood abruptly, making the rural dean abandon his wine and stand with him to mumble a thanksgiving. Helen drifted over to Melville and Mr Vaughn followed the lawyer into the panelled room that had so lately been the scene of tragedy.

The young man produced papers and books on which he was working. 'And this is the inventory of books that might have a high value,' he said.

'You were ordered to do this work?'

Mr Vaughn flushed. 'No, sir. I thought it fitting, and Lord Altone allowed me a free hand. I like to have everything documented so that I know exactly what is on these shelves, and in the case of valuable books, they might need safer keeping.'

The lawyer nodded. He began to think that the young woman would be guarded by at least four honest people in the old house. 'I am impressed, sir. I shall return in a month to see your progress and to check the accounts. You have a sacred duty here, Mr Vaughn and I don't mean just bricks and mortar and books.'

'I know, sir. I will do everything in my power to help Lady Charmian.' Mr Vaughn smiled. 'She is fortunate to have an affectionate older woman to care for her at this time. The Lady Altone is the perfect choice to teach her all the social graces.'

'That's as maybe,' said the lawyer, dryly. 'Time will tell, but remember that you have a sacred trust.'

Charmian was waiting by the door and ran to ring for the carriage, looking like a child and delighted to serve in even this simple way for someone she trusted and for whom she cared as a friend.

'Come, Mr Vaughn, we can wave from

the stables.'

He followed her, thinking that there were two women in the house, and each one held some part of his devotion, but he was now bound closely to the young mistress of the manor and must make his account to the lawyer, making her interests a priority above all else.

He made a mental note to speak to the stable lad about the state of the harness, and as he would now be in charge of the running of Hornbeam Manor, he must make the servants know that he expected them to come to him for orders.

The horse that Melville rode the previous night had cast a shoe and the groom was poulticing the hoof. Mr Vaughn squared his shoulders. Life might be easier in many ways, but even with his increased status, some aspects would be difficult.

Meanwhile the lawyer settled back into his seat in the carriage as the coachman drew into the side of the lane to allow another coach to pass. The windows were hidden by curtains, but Mr Lanyon pursed his lips as he recognized the coat of arms on the sparkling door. He was suddenly cold. What could the Duke of Shalfleet, the notorious libertine, want in this part of Somerset? The lane led only to the tollgate and on to Hornbeam Manor and three small farms.

Not Charmian, please God, he prayed. No, that was ridiculous as the duke had never set eyes on the girl. So would Lady Altone welcome him? That was more likely, her and the young puppy with a taste for high living, gambling, foppish cravats and silk waistcoats. He looked grimly ahead. It was time he sent an agent to obtain news from Bath and to watch who came to the manor, and he hoped that Jack Vaughn was man enough to protect Charmian from that precious bunch of ne'er-do-wells who flocked round Lady Altone, and from the attentions of such men as the Duke of Shalfleet.

'Drive on, man! What have you in harness? Goats or donkeys?' he said with fury that had its roots in fear.

Four

The grey cat streaked across the gravel drive, as the coach stopped by the deep porch of the manor after swaying round the central flower bed and sending up showers of loose gravel. A footman jumped down to fix the steps so that His Grace could alight without effort.

Edwin, Duke of Shalfleet, paused to survey the fine avenue of trees leading to the park, and the vista beyond to the River Avon, winding away to the Vale of Keynsham. It was a fitting place for Lady Altone, he thought, and his smile reflected the pleasure he anticipated on meeting her again.

He ignored the footman and the coachman as they led the horses away to the stables, and so missed the curious gaze of a girl half hidden by a tree at the end of the path. He walked with all the arrogance of one who by reason of rank and personal charm knows he must be welcome, and even seen to be conferring an honour on any household he thought fit to visit.

Prudence smoothed her apron with agitated fingers. This was the third visit the duke had made to the manor, but the first since Lord Altone was killed by an unknown hand. She bobbed and ran back to the house, calling to a maid that her ladyship had a visitor and she must be told at once.

'M'Lord,' said Dermot, holding back the front door. The duke strode past him with a curt nod of recognition. 'My Lady has been informed, M'Lord. May I offer some refreshment?' Dermot ushered him into the lower drawing room, a lovely salon where formal visitors were admitted as soon as they arrived. The wide windows looked out on to a landscaped park with carefully chosen trees and soft banks of flowering shrubs. The sun made the gilt chairs seem almost too fragile for use in the elegant rose and eau de Nil room. The duke smiled faintly, picked up a book from the French sidetable and put it down again carelessly as if he had every right to be there, to touch whatever he fancied and to be thoroughly at ease.

'Nothing, my man. Just be good enough to tell Lady Altone that I have come to convey my condolences in person.' He glanced at Dermot as if he wanted to read his mind. 'Your master, how did he die?' It sounded a careless remark, tinged with curiosity as if it didn't really concern him. 'There have been many conflicting reports and I wish to know the truth of it.'

'He did not die, Your Grace. He was foully murdered.' Dermot held his gaze steady, not intimidated by the aristocratic face with the penetrating eyes. He wondered where there could be any other eyes as calculating and coldly blue.

The duke scrutinized him with greater interest, a sardonic smile on his full mouth. 'And was that not death? As much a death as lying in his bed?'

'No, sir,' Dermot said, stubbornly. 'It was not the death for my master. He deserved a better end than to be stabbed in his own house by a drunken rascal.'

'I see that he had good friends and loyal servants.'

'Aye, sir. Loyal and true and more than willing to avenge his death, come the day when we find the sword that killed him.' He almost expected the duke to laugh, but went on: 'He will be found, Your Grace. Make no mistake, he will be found.'

'Come now, my good man, you cannot make such a vow. You said that he was killed by a passing thief, a scroundrel in his cups, did you not? Where were you? Were you there when the fatal blow was struck? Was there anyone who saw the assailant?' He looked away as if he found Dermot's steady gaze importunate, and produced an onyx snuff box from a silk pocket. He took a pinch of snuff with a flourish wasted on Dermot and placed it in the dip of his thumb.

Dermot watched him without moving, silent although the duke paused for a reply, the snuff still balanced, and as he looked at the manservant's face, the snuff drifted down on to the frilled cravat, unheeded.

'What did you say?' the duke asked.

'I said nothing, Your Grace. There is nothing to say. I was not there and I can think of nobody who saw the crime. The Runners have been here but they gave us no answer and left us as much in the dark as we were before they upset the household.'

His Grace took more snuff, sniffed and made great play with a lace handkerchief.

'Was nothing seen? Nothing said in the servants' hall?' He laughed. 'Surely the servants have their own ideas? I have yet to find a house where the servants know less than their masters of what happens within the establishment.' He had the air of one confiding in an equal. 'You must know much of what happened here. My own servants know far more of my family affairs than is good, at times.'

The sudden warmth and bonhomie made Dermot wonder if, under the arrogant exterior, there might be someone in whom he could confide. Surely a man with the duke's wealth and intelligence could be someone in whom he could put trust to advise him what to do. The button that he had found in the library on the night of the murder and the scrap of lace was still his secret and was heavy on his mind. The lace was of such good quality that it could never have come from the wrist of a vagrant drunkard.

He looked at the duke's raiment, the coat edged with gold and frogged with velvet, cuffs agleam with gold buttons and lace wrist frills spilling like a froth of cobwebs, light and as fine as that other lace. He opened his mouth to speak of the button but the door was thrust open and the duke turned to greet Helen.

She stood in the doorway with the shadows of the hall behind her and the sun touching her hair, making it seem like spun gold. She was exquisite in white silk taffeta, with a black shawl of finest cashmere over her shoulders. In mourning, she was more beautiful than in her bright ball gowns, and the simple lines of her dress lent her an air of fragility that was almost virginal.

The duke seized her hands and kissed the scented fingers. Dermot saw the coarsening of the duke's face as he looked at Helen and he decided that it was as well to say nothing of his find. Some instinct told him that the fewer people who shared his confidence, the safer it would be for him and perhaps for others in the house. He slipped from the room and closed the door after him. He had noticed the shape of the duke's hands and knew them to be sensual and full of power. There was self-indulgence and something destructive: the hands were soft and pampered, but strong, with thick thumbs and the high mounts of Venus hinted at lust.

He had also glimpsed the face of his master's widow, free of sorrow and even a pretence of pain, but filled only with the excitement and pleasure that a woman has when wooed by a very important suitor. She had all the triumph of a woman who had made an incomparable conquest.

Helen curtseyed gracefully, with elegance rather than the respect due to a man of such rank, and she left her hand resting easily in his. 'You do us much honour, Your Grace,' she said formally, then whispered, 'I have missed you, Edwin.'

He stepped back when Prudence entered the room with a silver tray and fine porcelain filled with delicacies.

'Will you take tea with me, Your Grace,' Helen asked, dismissing Prudence with a curt nod and indicating that the footman should close the door after them. 'I shall pour the tea,' Helen said before Prudence left. 'Your visit gives me great pleasure, in my time of grief,' she said.

Prudence found her husband outside the door. 'What is it, Dermot? Not listening at doors?'

'No, I want to know nothing of what goes on in there,' he said contemptuously. 'The master not cold and she acts as if he never existed.' He clenched his hands.

'I know,' Pru said soothingly. 'There now, it's over and what can we do? The poor soul is at rest and we have our duties to do.'

'Our duty is to find who killed him!'

'No, my dear, we have important matters to consider. We have our dear Lady Charmian to protect from such as they are.'

'That we'll do for as long as she wants us, but we must take on the task of doing what is right by my master.'

'Sooner or later, it will be done. No man escapes his fate, husband. Truth will out when the good Lord decides, but now I have other things to do.' She picked up a tray from the hall table. 'I wish my lamb would eat, but she even refuses tea and muffins. Can you remember how she loved to eat muffins when she had tea with her father?'

She took tea to the library where Mr Vaughn was sitting high on the oaksteps, examining a large volume bound with heavy leather. He barely noticed Prudence when she called to him to take his tea. He saw the door open and shut, but didn't notice it open again, closing once more, softly.

'All right,' he said brusquely. 'I promise I'll not let it spoil again as I did yesterday. Pray pour me a cup and I'll be there as soon as I've noted this volume.'

He heard the chink of china and the rasp of sugar tongs and he closed the book. He came down the steps still holding the book and went to the bureau to make a note in the ledger where the new inventory was being amassed. Only then did he turn to the window seat and the tray on the small table. 'I beg your pardon,' he began, as he saw who it was had poured him his tea.

Charmian smiled. 'Do you forgive me, sir? I have stolen one of your muffins. I wanted no tea until I saw Pru with your tray and was suddenly hungry, so she brought more and another cup.' She bit into the muffin and laughed when the butter escaped from the sides. 'Oh, she will put in far too much butter, but they are quite delicious,' she said. She handed the dish to him and he took one while she poured more tea into the delicate cups.

Mr Vaughn was relaxed and found a pleasant diversion in her company. He was pleased to see how easily she talked when alone with him. Soon, they were chuckling over the illustrations in a book for children and the pictures of gremlins and goblins.

The cat purred between them on the window seat. 'Why call him Kavanagh?' asked Mr Vaughn.

A cloud passed over the girl's face, dimming her laughter. 'A dear friend, now dead, brought him from Ireland and my father said the cat was a real Irishman, gay and independent and very handsome. Such green eyes and such dignity, so we called him Kavanagh.' She touched the man's sleeve. 'Thank you for loving my father. There are servants here who loved him too, but I have few people to whom I can really talk and I am lonely.'

Jack Vaughn smiled tenderly, oddly moved by the slight gesture of trust. 'Dear child,' he said, 'you are wrong to feel lonely. There were many who loved him.' He looked at her reproachfully. 'What of Lady Altone? So new a bride to lose her husband. She told me of her grief and how much you mean to her. She wants nothing more than your happiness and is willing to bury her own sorrow to make your coming of age a success. She confided that she told the lawyer her intentions and persuaded him to let her take charge of the preparations.'

'She told you that?' Charmian drew away. 'Of course, you were not there when the will was read and my father's wishes made clear.'

He seemed puzzled. 'But Lady Altone is to prepare you, is she not?'

'That is true, sir, but you are mistaken if

you believe that my stepmother cares for me.'

'Have you given her the chance to prove it? I know of her grief that you are cold towards her. My Lady is shy ... she told me so.' He saw that she was troubled and took her hand in his. 'But if you need help or are lonely, I am here. I gave my word to the lawyer that I would protect your interests above all else, but it goes deeper, Lady Charmian. I want to help. Come into the library whenever you have time to spare. I need assistance with these books.' He smiled. 'Work is good when the soul is lonely.' He glanced at the well-stocked shelves. 'There is enough work to keep us occupied for several weeks.'

They sat talking until the gong sounded to remind them to dress for dinner and Mr Vaughn was reluctant to have the afternoon and evening end so soon. Now that his position was one of importance, he dined with the family as of right, but first he carefully locked away the inventory, as he'd discovered a few very valuable volumes and needed to have true descriptions of them safely locked in a drawer.

He hurried to change and thought how good it had been to see Charmian smile and relax in his company. Even if she didn't appreciate her good fortune in having Lady Altone as her stepmother, she was a dear child, a sweet ... disturbing child.

At dinner, Charmian smiled and enjoyed the food more than she had since her father's murder. Helen was witty and looked lovely, Melville was very attentive and Mr Vaughn regarded her with pleasure, so she felt happier.

The duke had left after two hours with Helen, and a brief but amicable conversation with Melville, offering him a place at his table the next day in the Assembly Rooms in Bath. Melville was elated, knowing that it was an honour to be taken under the patronage of such a powerful man. He plied Charmian with sweetmeats and insisted that she drink chocolate with him in the orangery, watching the moon rise over the dusky fields.

In the soft light, she saw only his silhouette, aglow with the colours of his elaborate coat. In this setting, after good food and more wine than she had ever drunk at one sitting, it was easy to believe that everyone loved her.

Melville talked of the fine dresses of the Assembly Rooms and the elegant gentlemen who gambled for vast sums of money. He made it sound very romantic and was skilled in painting a picture of a perfect society where everyone laughed, was witty and clever and all ladies were beautiful.

'I would never be the toast of anywhere, leave alone Bath,' Charmian said wistfully. 'I have but a year to prepare and I feel like a country bumpkin.' She looked up at him, her throat white aginst the delcate mauve fichu, and her eyes were troubled. 'I am afraid, Melville,' she said. He held her hand and kissed it fervently, and she didn't take it away. Helen joined them, looking pleased that her brother was making such progress with the young heiress.

'Who is afraid?' asked Helen laughing. 'Not you, Charmian. You have nothing to fear. You have ... so much.' She glanced at Melville. 'I assure you that with our help, you will have everything you desire, as well as your present position, your wealth and your pretty face. She is indeed pretty, Melville?' He smiled and bowed low, and Charmian felt her colour rising.

This was ridiculous! Yesterday, she had distrusted them, but surely Jack Vaughn, who she trusted, was right? Helen was being charming and Melville had stayed at the manor just to entertain her. Her heart warmed towards them.

'You will help me?' she begged.

Helen exchanged a look of ironic humour with her brother. 'We shall do all that is necessary for all our sakes,' she said.

'Perhaps Charmian would like to be presented earlier,' said Melville. 'Would you like that? The Duke of Shalfleet has offered me his patronage and I could ask him to enter your name for presentation in Bath, unless you want to wait for a London court? The Prince comes here for soirées and concerts for a season this autumn, to Bath.'

Helen stiffened, and although she forced a smile, her voice was hard. 'That will be too soon, Melville. You must not forget my period of mourning.' She sighed. 'One word of warning, Charmian. Although I am reluctant to say this. I'd rather you did not appear when the Duke of Shalfleet visits the manor. Of course, he knows that I have a lovely stepdaughter to who I am devoted, who is also an heiress. This is a delicate matter, my dear. Although the duke is a good friend to my brother, and because of that I entertain him here, he is not the kind of man that your father would like you to know intimately. He is married and it would be a melancholy day if he caused you any embarrassment. Believe me, I take my trust very seriously, and wish to protect you from such creatures.'

Melville smiled maliciously. His sister had no intention of letting His Grace set lecherous eyes on Charmian. He said gently, 'Charmian, I give my word that the noble duke shall never trouble you. I am your slave.' His lips on her hand had a lingering contact and a thrill unlike any that Charmian had experienced went through her fingers as she saw his eyes darken with something more than courtly charm. She blushed and accepted his homage, aware only of his warmth and his masculine good looks.

As she went to her room, she saw Jack Vaughn coming from the library. He was handsome too in his well-cut evening coat and his hair curling as if he had run worried hands through the thick locks. She rubbed the hand that Melville had kissed and thought with something akin to resentment that Jack Vaughn was too busy to kiss her hand and to tell her she was pretty.

I am not a child, she thought. He treats me as such and yet he cannot be more than a few years older than I am.

He walked along to the small salon without seeing her and Charmian pouted and ran to her room. He acts as old as Mr Lanyon and I am not a child! She no longer had the feelings of a child, she realized.

She flung open the door of her room and Debbie rose to meet her and help her to bed. As she brushed the shining hair, Debbie listened to the stories told second-hand of the wonders of Bath and the glittering society there. She could hear Melville's views and influence coming through the light chatter and her affectionate soul was troubled. She watched the glowing face with misgiving. Charmian was so young and vulnerable after living a cloistered existence in Wales. Pray God they don't turn her head and take away the simple happiness she knew after the sorrows of the past few weeks.

Five

Life returned to normal at Hornbeam Manor and it gradually seemed as though Lord Altone was not lying in the family vault but was away on a long visit to the estate in Wales. Charmian was instructed in the intricacies of the court curtsey and shown how to handle a train on her gown, to wear flowers and to carry posies with grace and ease. She was fitted for ball dresses and riding habits made in rich fabrics from special designs, and taught about food and wine and all the minutiae of court etiquette.

Charmian found it exciting and she learned fast, developing a poise that made Melville think that if he married her, he would be fortunate in many ways that had nothing to do with her wealth. He found to his surprise that he looked forward to their meetings and card games, finding her youth and exuberance refreshing after the sophistication of Bath. He began to wonder if he wasn't at least half in love with her, and his charm and attentiveness made Charmian forget her first impression of him. Debbie grew tired of hearing his name.

Mr Vaughn was busier than he'd ever been. His responsibilities grew as he took on more and more of the administration of the estates under the careful authority of Mr Lanyon, who quizzed him regularly about official business and the health and well-being of the young heiress, insisting that Jack Vaughn must give some time to her, even if his other duties were pressing.

'I need no instructions in that direction, sir,' said Mr Vaughn. 'I remember her father too well to want her lacking for company and healthy pursuits suitable to a young lady in my care.'

'Humph! You are a little young to be her self-appointed guardian.' The shaggy eyebrows came together. 'But I trust you as I'd trust no other man. You are loyal and kind and can have no thoughts of any relationship other than the one you have now, as you have no fortune, no high position and no title.' It was plain speaking that made the young man flush with annoyance.

'My family is noble, sir. An accident of birth made me a younger son and yet my blood is as good as any who bear the title.' He drew himself up proudly, and Mr Lanyon felt a pang of regret that this man could never be acceptable as a suitor for Charmian. He had matured into a very handsome man, whose quiet manners held the respect of everyone in the estates and whose word was law and recognized as such in the areas of work where he held complete authority. 'I have no aspirations to Hornbeam Manor, but I am fond of the child and can give her instruction that she can have from no dancing master or the fops who say they educate her.' His tone was bitter and Mr Lanyon wondered if he fully understood his own feelings.

'The riding goes well?'

Jack Vaughn relaxed. 'It does indeed. Mr Melville sleeps late after his evenings in Bath and Lady Charmian is ready early to take the air. We ride each fine morning and she works with me in the library if the weather is inclement.' He frowned. 'She rides with Melville at times, but I am glad to note that Lady Altone does not allow them to ride alone in the carriage.'

'So I should think! But she does need to go out and enjoy the countryside.'

'I take her with me when I visit farriers and corn chandlers in Bath and in the villages where the manor has property, but Debbie comes with us.' He smiled, as he recalled the innocent pleasure that they all derived from such outings and the warmth of friendship between Charmian and himself. She seemed to depend on his company and sought his opinion on matters that were in no way his concern but which he gravely treated as important, sometimes wondering why her cheeks were pink when he sounded too much like Mr Lanyon.

'Keep her in your care, my boy. She will need you more, not less as time goes by, until she is safely married.'

Jack Vaughn watched the carriage leave and was suddenly sad. If Charmian married, then it would be her husband who would take over the husbandry of the estates. He walked briskly back to the library. That was a small matter and well into the future. He saw Charmian waving from the gallery above the stairs. She was laughing and he noticed how her muslin dress fell softly from the low neckline of the simple gown, revealing the promise of a swelling bosom. He lifted a hand in greeting and a pang of something more than loyal guardianship made his face pale. She would marry some elegant, titled rake, a friend of the duke's, and be lost to him for ever.

'Mr Vaughn! I have been looking for you. I need to select more ribbons from the shop on Poulteney Bridge, or so Lady Altone tells me. I thought we had enough to dress ten maypoles, but she insists that I go today.'

'You will take the small carriage?'

Her eyes sparkled. 'Melville said that he would take me in the four-in-hand and get there as quick as light.'

'That is impossible!' He couldn't stop the words or hide his displeasure. 'Mr Lanyon would be vexed if you travelled in that manner. You would be alone with the driver, and the four-in-hand is no vehicle for a lady, driven as Mr Melville would do.'

Silently, he blessed the lawyer's authority but knew that the opinions he voiced in such vigorous terms were his own.

'Then you shall take me, sir! For I will go to Bath today.' Her eyes were bright and she was agitated. 'You treat me as a child, and yet I am to come out in a little while and then I may drive alone if I wish, and share my carriage with whosoever I choose to have with me.'

'You do not wish me to ride with you?'

They met halfway up the stairs and she was two steps above him, bringing her face level with his. She seemed uneasy at their sudden proximity. 'Of course I do. I didn't mean ... I only felt...' The words died away and they stared, each wondering at the beauty of the other. He breathed deeply and stood aside.

'You will take me, Mr Vaughn?' A hint of the studied coquetry that she had learned slipped into her tone as if she needed to hide her true feelings.

'If that is your wish,' he replied formally. 'But I suggest the other carriage as I need to take it for a small repair that can be done while you choose silks, so it will be convenient to be in Bath today. Tell Debbie we shall leave after luncheon.'

He walked from the library and she looked at his retreating back, admiring the width and strength of his shoulders and his easy unrehearsed elegance.

She watched until the library door closed. He had been different and she experienced a sudden panic that he would soon no longer share the silly jokes and enjoy the simple pleasures with her that Helen and

Melville despised. She sighed as the dressmaker arrived for even more fittings.

Helen was a hard taskmistress, but a very competent teacher, and Charmian knew that she'd be free to go to Bath while Helen entertained her own friends in her boudoir, drinking tea or chocolate and playing cards, as she couldn't attend the soirées in Bath while in official mourning. Today, Helen was almost too eager for Charmian to leave for Bath as soon as luncheon was over, as if she expected a guest who Charmian must not meet.

After luncheon, she waited with Debbie for the carriage and Mr Vaughn. 'We are early,' he said with satisfaction. 'We shall have time to drive through the villages and perhaps enjoy a glass of milk at one of the farms.' He wore a new jacket of soft dark cloth which made him appear very masculine, if a trifle sombre. It was a correct costume for his role as escort to the lady of the manor and as he handed Charmian into the carriage, she wondered why the men who came now to pay homage to Helen wore such bright colours, unless, perhaps, they had no masculinity and wore the brightness to hide any deficiencies.

The coachman flicked his whip and the

horses trotted briskly down the drive to the wide gateway. A flurry of dust almost made the lead horse rear. Melville, in a dashing riding habit and a black tricorne hat, flashed by with a derisive wave of one hand and a glance of venom towards Jack Vaughn.

The coachman swore and Mr Vaughn leaned out of the window to make sure that no harm had been done to the horses or the leather traces. His mouth was set in a firm line of displeasure. This was becoming too often the exhibition that Melville showed, and the horse so driven would be returned to the stables winded and sweating, left carelessly with a groom, as Melville went into the house unheeding of the stable boys who had to calm the animal and make sure that no harm had been done.

'He rides well,' Charmian said. She had seen only the flying figure and not the bad horsemanship.

'He rides fast,' Mr Vaughn said and she smiled. He was envious of the man who could take any horse he wanted, by right of being Helen's brother and not because he was employed by the estate. 'But I have seen the beasts when he returns,' Vaughn said.

She eyed him keenly. He was not envious; he was concerned.

'Surely he must love horses?'

'He loves riding them. That is quite different.'

Debbie clucked her approval. It was time that someone raised a voice against Mr Melville and his careless habits. She thought that Lady Altone allowed him to use the manor too much as his home and lavished money and luxury on him, while Lady Charmian was dazzled by his looks and fine manners.

Melville rode in the direction of Bath, and soon they saw his racing mount breast the hill ahead and vanish down into the valley. Charmian bit her lip. That hill was too steep to take so fast. Her father would never have allowed it, and she was suddenly silent. She missed her father, but for increasing periods she no longer grieved and it saddened her. The coach turned into a farmyard where the view was good and the smell of newly mown hay reminded Charmian of times when she had tossed the drying grass and set the stooks with the haymakers, leaving them to dry in the summer sun. It had been good as a child on the Welsh estates. She sighed. So much was happening to her, too fast for comfort and she only half-wanted to be the toast of Bath.

'Melville was cross when I told him that I was driving to Bath with you,' she said and smiled to charm the stern face beside her.

'So, in anger he whips his horse and rides like the devil,' Jack Vaughn said.

Charmian bit her lip and looked out of the window, hurt that he believed she saw nothing wrong in Melville's actions. 'He rides carelessly,' she conceded, 'but he does care about me enough to make sure I am entertained and never bored.'

'And is that a duty?' The dark eyes seemed to bore into her and she looked away. 'Surely that is a pleasure that many gentlemen will vie to take once you are of age, Lady Charmian. There are other men with better prospects and better blood than Mr Melville who will pursue you in the hope of a moment of your time.'

She glanced at him again. He was tense as if in the thrall of a deep emotion that was not anger.

'Melville is my stepuncle,' she said, defiantly. 'He is vastly entertaining and owes much to Lady Altone and I am fond of him.'

Jack Vaughn flushed. 'I beg your pardon. It is just that I have a duty and must see that you reach your debut without your head being turned by flattery and pretty manners.'

'So, with you, sir, it is a duty,' she mocked.

'No, you are quite aware that I enjoy your company,' he replied stiffly. 'But you are about to enter a new world where I can no longer protect you as I would wish. Even Debbie will have to let you go at times and it is possible to feel very much alone, under the bright lights and in the midst of glittering company. If only I could be there,' he added softly.

'La, sir, I think you hanker after the salons,' she said in her best imitation of Helen at her most provocative.

'Not the salons,' he said and firmly turned her attention to a cart full of hay on which were perched a small girl and boy. He wondered if he could fulfill his obligations to the lawyer for much longer.

Her face glowed with gentle laughter as the children waved and she kissed her gloved hands to them as the cart turned away. The tension broke and Debbie seemed oblivious to everything but the pleasure of the day's outing. With Mr Vaughn in the carriage, she left the conversation to the two handsome young people. She saw the changing expressions on their faces and sighed. If only Mr Vaughn was a suitable match for her dear lamb, life would be good indeed. She tried not to think of the man and woman who had done so much to alter the atmosphere and events at Hornbeam Manor and prayed that Mr Vaughn would stay to protect her mistress from... She couldn't tell what, but sensed a fate that could bring sorrow if Lady Helen and Melville had control.

The afternoon passed quickly, with Charmian buying more than she needed and Mr Vaughn concluding his business and finding time to browse in one of the bookshops on Poulteney Bridge, close to the shops where Charmian examined silks. He spoke to the proprietor and asked the value of one or two of the titles he had discovered in the library, taking care not to mention where he had seen them or who owned them, as Bath and cities where wealthy people took their pleasures also held rogues who looked for easy pickings.

Charmian was reluctant to return home, as the late afternoon sun shone over golden fields and she longed to run free as she had done in Wales.

Mr Vaughn smiled indulgently, feeling decidedly safer with this child than with the lovely young woman. 'We can take tea with the farmer's wife,' he said, and the coach was driven into a familiar farmyard where Charmian ran ahead and was almost lost in the enveloping embrace of the woman whose family had been persuaded to follow Lord Altone from Wales to serve him again.

Soon they were chattering and eating fresh griddle cakes and farm butter, then Charmian changed into a cotton smock belonging to the farmer's daughter and picked up a basket for blackberries, leaving Debbie to drink more tea.

Jack Vaughn shared her sense of freedom and they picked and laughed over the tartness of some of the berries. Charmian was happier than she'd been for weeks and hummed to herself. She ran to the man who regarded her with devotion when he thought she couldn't notice, and he carried the baskets back to the farmhouse.

'We must go now,' he said gently, unwilling to break the spell.

'Oh, no!' She looked up pleading, and put her hands in his.

'Your hands are stained,' he said as he turned them over to show her the purple patches. 'What will Lady Altone say if she sees you like this?' His tone was light but he wanted to kiss the grubby little hands.

She drew away, suddenly pale. 'Let us go

back, then,' she whispered, and when she came out to the carriage dressed in her own clothes, with well scrubbed hands, she was once more the young lady destined for great occasions. 'If you hurry now, we might even see the elusive duke,' she said. He looked startled. 'I am sent away whenever he is expected,' Charmian said calmly. 'Didn't you know?'

'His Grace comes to see Mr Jaspern,' Vaughn said. 'If he was riding this afternoon, then the duke could not be expected today.'

'My dear Mr Vaughn, I think it is you who is the child that you seem to think I am!' Charmian tossed her head, knowing that she was angry that he should have such an innocent belief in Lady Altone. The fact that Helen worked hard and made everything easy for her to learn how to act as a lady of fashion did nothing to still the gossip of servants and what Charmian gleaned from Debbie. The duke came often and stayed late, even when Melville was not at home.

As if to show that she was right, they saw the coach bearing the ducal arms leaving the manor. Jack Vaughn frowned when they stopped in front of the main entrance, in a slowly subsiding cloud of dust raised by the duke's carriage.

She saw and enjoyed his discomfort. 'Remember we have guests tonight, Mr Vaughn. You have blackberry juice on your cheek.' She reached up and wiped it away with a cambric handkerchief she took from her bosom. He crushed the soiled square in his hand and kept it, but could say nothing as Melville came slowly from the stables, gave them a sharp look and disappeared into the house without more than a forced smile for Charmian.

Melville ran to Helen's boudoir. 'Why do you allow her to be taken out by Vaughn?' he said. He dropped his riding crop on the table and pulled off his cuffed riding gloves which fell to the floor.

Helen regarded him coolly. She looked flushed and very lovely, her eyes sparkling with the excitement of lovemaking with her illustrious visitor. She smiled. It was unfair that she could indulge her sexual appetite while Melville must curb his desires and be circumspect as far as Charmian was concerned. 'I know you want her, and I am glad. I think that if you are patient and play her carefully, she will come to you, willingly.'

'Patience?' He walked restlessly across to

89

the window and back again.

'Yes, my dear, patience!' Her smile died. 'I have watched you with her and I held my breath last evening when I thought you might sweep her into your arms in the upper gallery.' She laughed. 'I see everything, so be careful. You ride too fast. Keep her on a light rein or she may yet bolt. Any display of passion now will frighten her. She is not one of your doxies from London, to be taken without a lengthy wooing.'

'But she is ready! When we are together, she is aware of me. We could elope and damn the lawyers!'

'No!' Helen looked alarmed. 'The time is not ripe. We must be careful and wait until she has been presented, then we can arrange a marriage. There must be no suspicion of scandal or seduction. We must be able to face the lawyers with a girl hopelessly in love with you and then even Mr Lanyon will have no power to prevent a wedding.'

'Waiting, waiting, waiting! Playing the fool and playing at cards, with no gambling.'

'You were content last week.'

'That was then.' He turned away and paced the room again. 'I sat with Boswell Martin last night at the duke's table.'

Helen paled. Boswell Martin was a man of

noble birth but with an infamous reputation. He was reckless and completely ruthless, using his position and wealth to ruin young bucks who dared to pit their wits against his. Ugly rumours of early morning duels and at least two suicides made the rounds of society gossip and it was only the patronage of the duke and the Prince Regent himself that spared Boswell Martin from the law.

'I had an unquiet night,' Melville said sulkily, as if it was the fault of his sister.

'And now?' Her voice shook.

'I lost all the money you gave me.'

She gazed into the mirror and arranged her hair, adding jewels to the elaborate setting. More jewels hung from her neck and arms and her delicate fingers were ablaze with diamonds, given to her freely in the first blissful months of honeymoon.

'I lost all!' he stressed.

'I must think,' she said. 'Go now and dress for dinner. We have guests and you must smile and act the gallant.'

'I need money now.' He eyed the gems that shone brightly on her white skin.

'You know, Mel, that I have no control over the estate. I have been more than generous. I even gave you the money put aside for the dressmakers. I dare not give you more before the lawyer comes to check the books. I must present a true account or he will withold everything and I shall be ruined.'

Melville gave a snort of anger.

'I want to give you everything you desire, Mel, but you are too free with money. Can it not wait until Charmian brings you a fortune? Until then, you have no status in this house and could be asked to leave if she turned against you. She could send me to the Dower House in Wales, heaven help me!' Her eyes were cold. 'That prospect frightens me more than anything. All those awful provincials! I dream of those wide, wet, empty hills and the complete lack of everything that makes life bearable. I haven't worked so hard that I intend to be deprived now by you or anyone.' She stood and came closer, speaking in a low voice so that they could not be overheard. 'When my husband was killed, it was a great shock ... but also a great relief. I am very grateful, because—'

'Grateful, madam? Because of what? Are you telling me you wanted him dead?'

Helen stared. '*You* ask me that? You knew of my liason with Edwin and that my husband had discovered it...' Her voice faltered and she clutched his arm, her calm shattered. 'If you did not kill him, then who...?'

They stared at each other aghast. 'Sister! Do you think me capable of that?' His bitter voice cut through her consternation.

'But if not you,' she whispered, 'who was in the house that night? It must have been you! I saw mud on your boots and you were fully dressed under your chamber robe. You panted as if you had been under great physical distress and I thought you had done this for me and to get Charmian for yourself.'

He shook his head slowly. 'Madam, I am innocent. I am not capable of murder. I have no stomach for swords or pistols.' His face was pale. 'That is what I face now if I do not pay my debts. I shall receive a visit from the seconds of one of the finest shots in Somerset. I did not kill your husband. On the night of his death, I was riding hard with an angry landowner at my heels. I lost him, praise be, two miles away and doubled back here from another direction.' He smiled. 'She was worth it at the time, but I no longer want such conquests. I lost them all in the eyes of my future wife. I left the horse in the spinney by the stream and walked back through the woods as I wanted no prying eyes to see my return in case it got back to the husband and his bully boys. I have no stomach for their rough justice.'

'She will not tell?'

'She knows neither my name or lodging. I was masked when I wooed her at a ball in Bath and, to preserve the romance, remained masked when we met later in a barn.' He laughed. 'It was all vastly entertaining.'

'I heard one horse and believed it to be yours. If not you, then some other gentleman rode that night when Charmian screamed. Was it a thief? Nothing was taken.'

Her face was drawn. Who but Melville knew of her liason with the duke? Was it an admirer who wanted to prevent her being dismissed to the Dower House? Who loved her enough to risk his life, or who was villain enough to need the scandal and would keep it quiet as a means to later blackmail?

Melville frowned. 'It could have been one of Shalfleet's men, although I can't see him confiding in a lackey. It would leave him open to danger. Does it matter? No one has approached us for money to still his tongue, and now you are a widow, you do as you please.' He laughed. 'Perhaps it was that calf-eyed man in the library. He has eyes for none but you and I know that Charmian is safe with him as he considers her to be half-child and the untouchable daughter of his old patron.' He tapped his silk-clad leg with ringed fingers. 'Who knows what that one would do for you, given the test?'

'No, not Jack Vaughn. He is a man of honour. He came to the scene stunned with real sorrow.' She considerd what had happened. He had taken Charmian to her room when she swooned and although he was strong and lithe, he was not a fighting man.

'No, not Jack Vaughn.' She regarded her brother with an insolent smile. 'I have no money for you and it seems my gratitude towards you was misplaced.' Melville looked at her with growing horror. 'It seems that another rid me of my husband.'

'You are inhuman! You wanted him dead! Perhaps it was a woman who killed him.'

Fear showed in her eyes. '*Never* say that again. *Never*, do you hear? If anyone heard that, we could be in mortal danger. It is not true, I swear it.'

His cynical smile had more assurance now. 'If I hinted that you trembled when you stood by me on the stairs and even that you hid the blood on your gown? Would anything save you, even if you are innocent? Why should I save you if you have no mercy on me?' he threatened.

He took her hand gently as if to raise it to his lips in salute, then held the hand in a crushing grip while he stripped away the rings. 'You owe me these for believing that I was capable of *that*!' he said, and flung her from him, leaving her weeping and nursing her bruised fingers. Melville thrust the rings into his pocket and slammed the door as he left her room.

He breathed deeply and composed his features. Charmian was in the upper gallery, dressed in pale grey dimity with velvet flowers of soft purple in her hair. He stopped, all anger evaporating.

Charmian's hands fluttered to her throat. 'Melville, what is wrong?'

'Nothing that concerns you, dear sweet Charmian.' He took her two hands and kissed them, then looked deeply into her eyes. 'Forgive me, I am late and am a little distraught. I have worries.'

'Melville, are we not friends? True friends? May I share your troubles as we share our good times?'

He took her sweet troubled face in his hands and brushed her lips with his. 'That is one of my troubles that soon you could soothe away at a touch, my dearest, dearest Charmian.'

Her heart beat faster and a pulse throbbed in her head, but she drew away. 'You must not, Melville! Oh, no!' Her eyes widened in an exquisite fear and he forgot the words of his sister.

His arms tightened and his lips sought hers in a kiss of such passion that her whole body trembled. He controlled himself and held her away.

'I love you, my darling,' he said. 'When you are presented, I shall ask you the question that hovers on my lips even now, as it has done since the first time I saw you.' His blue eyes flashed and he was very pale.

'Melville, you cannot be serious! All those lovely women you talk about in the Rooms. How can I compete with them? I am too young and inexperienced, too stupid for you.'

'If only I could take you now,' he whispered hoarsely. 'Charmian, my angel, say that you will remember this moment as a bond, and when the time is right, you will say yes?'

She drew back, remembering that his eyes were very like Lady Helen's when she was determined to have her own way. 'You go too fast, my dear,' she said. 'I have a lot to learn and I am confused.' The thrill of the kiss filled her with sensations of which she had only dreamed. Was this love? Was this the love such as her parents had shared? Behind the passion in his eyes she glimpsed something lacking of the tenderness her father had shown. There was something predatory and alien. 'Do not ask me such questions, Melville.' She leaned against the balustrade and he kissed her hands again. In the doorway of the library, she saw a man dressed immaculately in sober grey. He was looking up at the couple in the gallery with disbelief and horror on his face.

Melville saw him and smiled, grimly. It would do that puppy good to see that Charmian was at least half in love with Melville Jaspern, whose patron was the noble Duke of Shalfleet. If he gossiped about what he saw, so much the better. If Charmian had been kissed and compromised, it would do him no harm.

Charmian blushed and ran to her room, leaving the two men to stare at each other, like hostile stags at bay.

Charmian sat while Debbie brushed her hair and tied it back in a simple snood.

Melville had stirred her in a way that she found upsetting, but rather thrilling. She recalled the look of horror on Jack Vaughn's face and her heart beat painfully, as if he had caught her in some terrible act.

It is none of his business! she tried to convince herself. How dare he make her feel guilty. He had looked so stern and masterful. She jerked her head away from Debbie.

'Enough, Debbie, I must go down.'

She had to see if Mr Vaughn would smile at her again, if they could be friends and comfortable together once more. Would he want to come riding with her now? He must! It was his duty and she would make him do as she wanted even if he was angry with her. But she walked slowly, dreading any displeasure in his dark brown eyes.

Six

Charmian rubbed her aching temples with an attar of roses and Debbie smoothed the crumpled fichu so that the frill fell in a pale curve from her bosom and, once more, the lovely girl looked poised and exquisite. Her training with Helen had given her the ability to hide her true feelings in public, and when she appeared in the doorway of the salon, she adopted a slightly bored air that supposedly showed good breeding.

The other guests were in their places and Helen talked and laughed as if there were no dark corners in her mind. Melville gave Charmian a fond glance, secure in the memory of her yielding body close to his and the conviction that it would be only a short while before she would surrender to him completely, before other handsome rakes appeared on the scene. He certainly looked very handsome and the cut and splendour of his clothes made the casual observer forget the weakness of his chin and the dissolution that hinted would be in evidence in a year or so.

Jack Vaughn sat silent, left out of the conversation that centred on the gossip of Bath and he was unable to look directly at Charmian. His mind was full of confused thoughts. Surely his anger was rooted in disappointment? It could be nothing more, could it? The idea of Charmian permitting the liberty of Melville kissing her was enough to sadden any girl's guardian. Was it her wish that Melville was so bold? Vaughn sat tall on the gilt chair and wondered why it was so important to him. He stole a glance at the sweet curve of her cheek and the graceful fall of the delicate fabric at her bosom. He dismissed any idea of a deeper feeling and frowned as he sipped the fine wine from the Venetian glass.

I am bound to feel concern, he told himself. I would feel the same for a sister or cousin and certainly for the daughter of my patron and benefactor. Any vulnerable girl should be protected from such a popinjay.

He saw that Lady Helen had one hand hidden in the deep sleeve of her gauzy gown, but when she raised her glass, it was revealed and he saw the bruises. He was concerned lest she had suffered an accident or a deliberate injury. It was strange to conceal something caused by casual bruising, and she would mention it lightly as the result of her own carelessness, but he intercepted a glance between Helen and Melville and saw anger and almost hatred. It was a shock to read the same ruthlessness in Helen's eyes as blazed in those of her brother. For a moment, the aura of tender beauty vanished, the softness and helplessness and all that had ensnared him. How alike they are, he thought. Both handsome, with blue eyes now as hard as diamonds and full of defiant resolve as if they were at war.

Charmian laughed softly and he turned to look at her, recalling with a pang the innocence of their relationship when riding and working together in the library. Through the mist of infatuation he had felt for Lady Altone, came a glimmer of light, of self-knowledge and a warning that Charmian could suffer harm from the elegant brother and sister. No wonder the dour lawyer needed someone he could trust to look after her. He watched as dinner progressed and saw how they both made sure that Charmian was served well, and how they flattered her constantly.

They moved from the table to the smaller salon for cards and Helen kept her hand covered even when holding the cards. Footmen offered sweetmeats and wine, and Helen was falsely brilliant, witty and entertaining, but her eyes still held the chill of her encounter with Melville. He disappeared and the urgent clop of hooves came clearly through the summer night.

Charmian refused to play cards and walked into the orangery alone, glad to be away from the idle chatter. The air was warm and still and she sat in the open doorway, breathing in the sweet scent of stocks in the garden. A shadow across her vision made her start.

'May I?' a voice asked.

'Pray, be seated, Mr Vaughn,' she said.

He took the seat beside her on the bench and spread the skirt of his mulberry velvet coat with unwonted care. She blushed as she recalled what he had seen in the gallery and was thankful that the light was dim in the shadow of the vines. She wondered, almost resentfully, why she cared for the good opinion of Mr Vaughn. He was very fine tonight in the new coat and breeches, but not half as pretty as Melville, who had dined in a coat of pale blue with dark edgings and so much lace that it flew in a small cloud when he moved.

'How bright the moon shines,' she said at last to break the silence. She felt very much alone with the man at her side, and had never felt so when they were working together in the library with the door shut. Here she could see the shadows of the guests in the next room and could hear the music played on violin and harpsichord in the card room, so they were not alone.

She stood up, unable to stay in the fraught silence. 'The house is airless. Will you walk a little, Mr Vaughn?' Anything to break the constraint between them would be good. How she wished that Melville had not kissed her, or if he had, she wished that Jack Vaughn knew nothing of it. He offered his arm, but it was worse than sitting close to him. She laid a timid hand on his sleeve and was increasingly aware of his strength and nearness as they walked in the dark shadows cast by the tall yew trees into the rose garden.

Moonlight shone on the late blooms, turning the petals to silver. Jack Vaughn plucked a rose and put it to her face. The dew on the rose left a cold tear and he saw the drop and wondered if it was dew or a tear. He wanted to brush it away from the soft roundness of her cheek above the lifting corner of her mouth but he busied himself with his pocket knife, cutting more roses for her room.

'No!' she said as he handed them to her. 'I'm sorry, so sorry.' She shrank back. 'It's not that I don't want them. I love roses, especially those, but I can't touch them.'

'Charmian, what is it?' His stern face softened and he called her by her name as if she was a child again. He dropped the flowers on a bench and took her hands in his. They were cold and trembling.

'They are the roses that I saw on my father. They were on his face and all about him, pale petals. When they bloom in the garden, I can love them as he did. They were his favourite flowers and I can see why they are called White Moonlight.' She looked at the silver avenue of roses. 'In a bouquet, I cannot touch them as I see only his face again as it was that night, with the petals falling and the spilled water on ... the stain on the carpet.'

Vaughn put a strong and comforting arm round the shaking girl and led her to a seat, pushing the rejected roses into the shadow of the hedge. 'Dear little girl,' he said, and warmth and tenderness enfolded her, making all safe again. He brushed away her tears with a silk handkerchief.

She smiled mistily and dabbed her eyes, then handed back the silk square and watched him put it in his pocket as if it was a precious relic.

'Thank you,' she said. 'I'm glad you picked the roses. Although they upset me, in a curious way I feel better. Having seen them like that I shall not be afraid of them again. I shall use them, in time, to make me remember what is still hidden, and I can now enjoy their beauty.' She sighed. 'There is no risk of seeing them in the house as my stepmother will have them nowhere near her; perhaps because she was there, too, or perhaps...' She saw the question in his eyes. 'Because, have you not noticed? So many of his more prized and much loved belongings have been put aside out of sight as if she wants to be rid of his memory.'

'That can't be true.' She looked at him steadily, and the moonlight showed his sudden disquiet. He saw with sudden clarity that it was so. The collection of rapiers and muskets no longer hung in the gallery and the large portrait of Lord Altone, which had been in Helen's drawing room, had gone. All formerly welcome visitors were no longer invited unless they came with requests or on business, or were from important county families, who were not put off by the widow even if they were invited under sufferance, as they were too powerful to offend. The library was cluttered with Lord Altone's personal souvenirs that had been rejected, as if Helen need never enter that room again.

These facts, and the glimpse he'd had of the cold woman under the brilliance and charm, made Jack Vaughn silent. He placed Charmian's hand on his arm and walked her near the shrubs of the Italian garden and down to the lake. An undercurrent of unease filled his mind. Charmian in the moonlight was a slender wraith, young and lovely and wholly vulnerable. He was certain that Helen planned to persuade her to marry Melville and he was deeply shocked. How could Charmian sacrifice her life to a man like that?

He felt sick at the memory of the kiss he'd witnessed and her soft body pressed close to Melville's heart. At that moment, he knew that he cared deeply for the girl, and not because she was the daughter of his patron. His own background and blood was better than Jaspern's, but without a title and having no wealth, and no patron like the Duke of Shalfleet who had the friendship of the Prince Regent, he knew he had no chance against Melville.

A movement of swirling material among the trees told them that some guests were taking the air between games. One of the group was the worse for wine and he was laughing coarsely. He lurched forward, his eyes red, his smile offensive. 'Gad Sir, it's you! It's the silent man at dinner, the spectre at the feast and the stern conscience of us all; but a sly one for all that. Got the girl to yourself, have you? You sly devil, just the night for it ... moonlight and rose petals and all that. They love it, y'know. She's as pretty a peach as ever I picked and I envy you, sir.'

He moved forward and two men tried to pull him away, telling him to hold his tongue. Charmian was shaken and humiliated and clung to the strong arm that tried to thrust her behind him so that he could strike the insolent face. They pulled the man away and gradually Charmian felt the hard muscles of Vaughn's arm relax and she tucked her hand under it, looking up into his furious face.

'You must not, Mr Vaughn, even for me. You see? Nothing is the same. No man would dare insult a lady under this roof in my father's day.' Vaughn hugged her arm close to his side, quelling the desire to sweep her into his arms.

Charmian was thoughtful and sad. 'I am growing up fast and some of what I see I do not care for.' She glanced at the white face and the set lips and knew with relief that Jack Vaughn no longer thought of Helen as the lady without blemish who was working for the sole good of her stepdaughter.

Helen was all offended concern when Charmian returned to the house. She glanced anxiously at Jack Vaughn to see his reaction to the insult that Charmian had suffered. He gave her a brief smile. She did seem overly concerned as she suggested that Charmian might like to retire early and avoid the bibulous guests.

Charmian smiled goodnight and Jack Vaughn asked to be excused too as he had work to complete in the library. Helen's relief was obvious and he wondered why she wanted Charmian out of the way until he saw the leather trim on a discarded hat bearing the coat of arms of the duke's stables, which a lackey had left while he went to the kitchen for refreshment. Distant hoof beats came crisply to the ear and Melville arrived, throwing himself from his mount and handing him carelessly to a groom at the front door, before hurrying to his room to take off riding boots and top cloak. An air of expectancy filled the hall as carriage wheels approached and Jack Vaughn realized why Helen had wanted Charmian out of the way.

Vaughn left the library door open a little and hoped that Charmian wouldn't be curious about the new sounds, but there was no sign of Debbie so he could give her no warning.

Charmian had heard voices calling and the crunch of carriage wheels on gravel, but she thought the guests were leaving early. She walked along the gallery, wondering if the book she had begun to read in the library might be amusing enough to read before she went to bed. She hesitated at the head of the stairs, her hair loose but wearing the gown she'd worn at dinner. Her eyes were large and deep and her hair glowed russet under the soft lights. Dermot hurried across the hall, dressed in his smartest livery, and the outer doors were flung open wide.

Only then did Charmian know who was visiting Lady Helen so late, to play cards and later to remain in her boudoir until the small hours.

A tall man with broad shoulders stood against the light, his elegant legs clad in yellow silk stockings, his damask coat a deep claret and his lace exquisite. He took a step inside the hall, ignoring the smiling guests who lined the way to the salon but glanced up, aware of someone watching from above. He raised his head, his usual insolence gone in an expression of wonder and discovery as he saw a slender wonan with one dainty stockinged foot in a polished black calf pump, poised above the second stair. He followed the line of her leg to the thigh and lingered on the trim waist and the rise of her bosom. He wondered at the simple beauty of natural unclasped hair ... of such colour and thickness.

Charmian fled, overcome by the strange expression in the duke's eyes.

He took snuff and regained his poise before turning to the short rise of stairs at the side of the hall, which led to Helen's apartments. When Charmian peeped over the balustrade, the hall was empty and she hurried down to the library, wide-awake and knowing that sleep would be impossible.

'I am not tired,' she said when Jack Vaughn looked up in surprise. 'I am going to summon Debbie to bring me chocolate. Will you join me, Mr Vaughn?'

He left the piles of papers and books, and pulled on the bell rope, relieved to have Charmian under his care while the duke was in the house. The inventory was on the desk and he had added his list of valuable books, ready for the scrutiny of the lawyer on his next visit.

After an hour, the murmur of people leaving gave way to silence and Charmian was content to sip chocolate and to look at the books, afraid that she might see the duke again if she ventured from the library.

Melville, shut out of Helen's rooms, wandered into the library. The two men exchanged cold nods at first, then Melville seemed to make an effort to be pleasant. He asked intelligent questions about the valuable books, and in spite of his dislike of the man, Jack Vaughn couldn't conceal his enthusiasm for his work. He shared details that Charmian found fascinating, and Melville climbed the library ladder to examine more books that Vaughn mentioned, some decorated with wonderful illuminations and gold leaf, the life's work of monks from a humble holy order.

Charmian was delighted to see the two men so engrossed. She rang for more chocolate and almond biscuits, and claret for the gentlemen, and wondered if Melville needed some interest to turn him from the folly of gambling. She sat half asleep until she heard more carriage wheels and realized with a shock that it was after four in the morning. She stretched and said goodnight, safe in the fact that the duke had left. Melville yawned and Jack Vaughn packed away his inventory and snuffed the candles and lamps.

Melville lounged against the door, watching his movements, and frowned when he saw how closely locked the cabinets were before the librarian left the room. Jack Vaughn even threw back the curtains and checked that the windows were safe and the shutters bolted.

Charmian refused Debbie's sleepy offer to help her to bed, and when she lay in the darkness, she smiled. Growing up wasn't all bad. Two handsome men cared about her, in different ways, and she was friends once more with Mr Vaughn. She turned her mind from the duke's face when he came into her dreams.

Seven

Charmian slept late and missed her early ride with Mr Vaughn. There was no sign of Melville and Helen stayed in her rooms all day. A steady drizzle of rain robbed the garden of colour and the occupants of the manor of all amusements.

Charmian yawned with a mixture of boredom and the effects of a very late night and found herself looking forward to dinner, when at least there would be conversation to divert her.

She selected a pretty gown of soft turquoise, glad that she was no longer compelled to wear mourning, at least at home, and she went down to the library early, ready to chide Mr Vaughn for not being changed for dinner.

He glanced at the tall clock and smiled, sensing that she was bored. 'It's early,' he said.

'I have been alone all day,' she complained. 'You were away and Melville and Helen have not been to see me. We have had no visitors and it rained.' She looked out at the clearing sky. 'It will be fine tonight when I am asleep,' she said resentfully.

'But tomorrow it will be fit for riding, Lady Charmian,' he said.

'Yesterday, you called me Charmian,' she said and left him with his colour rising.

'May I take you in?' Melville asked. He appeared at the library doorway. 'My sister is waiting for us. Gad, what a boring day. I went into Bath and the rain spoiled the set of my cravat. Come now, Charmian, there are guests who you invited, friends of your father who insist on calling, and Helen wants you to entertain them.' He looked bored, but Charmian went eagerly to greet old friends, knowing once more the warmth of their feeling for her and her father. There were other guests, invited by Helen, who simpered among themselves and the table would be full that evening.

Mr Vaughn came down dressed with impeccable good taste, but soberly. His cravat was spotless but plain and his shirt unfrilled. Charmian went to his side, leaving the brightly dressed man who tried to gain her attention by talking of gaming and fashions and matters that no longer thrilled her with their novelty.

Melville followed her and said in a voice loud enough for all to hear, 'Have you consulted an expert about the value of those books, Mr Vaughn?' Vaughn frowned as if he resented Melville's interference in his work. 'I don't doubt your competence, sir. After the lecture you gave me last night on the value of certain books, I confess that I am very impressed by your knowledge, but it is customary to have a valuation, is it not?' His voice was relaxed and his face devoid of cupidity.

Mr Vaughn relaxed. 'As you know, I have the matter in mind as soon as I have finished listing them. I know the approximate value but I shall obtain another opinion so that it can be recorded in case of theft.'

'Theft?' Charmian said. 'Who would want to steal old books? An ordinary thief would pass them by for more easily sold jewels.'

'There are many wealthy collectors who would pay a great deal for such books and some would not query from whence they came. If the buyer is powerful and close to the Crown, even if the thief was discovered, the man might go free as there would be little proof as to the true ownership,' Vaughn said.

Charmian was horrifed. 'If a felony is proved, how can anyone escape the law, regardless of rank? Even titled people are tried by their peers.'

Jack Vaughn smiled bitterly. 'There are laws for the rich and influential and those for the poor,' he said. 'Only the poor and defenceless can expect ... justice, the justice of Newgate, the hulks and the gallows.'

'That is not entirely true,' Melville said. 'If a gentleman is taken after a dual, he is sent to the assizes as any highwayman or foot-pad.'

'That is a public matter,' Jack Vaughn said. 'But in dealing with art treasures, things are done in secret, and any hands involved are crossed with gold. Money makes morals, Mr Jaspern.'

'And what of murder?' Charmian asked softly. 'Rank should not protect a murderer.'

'The rich have fast horses,' said Jack Vaughn cryptically.

Helen looked thoroughly put out when the conversation at dinner continued to be of books. Melville wouldn't leave the subject alone and harped on the fact that the valuable books were an invitation to dishonesty.

'Already, the library window has been forced on the night of Lord Altone's murder, so why could it not be done again to steal books? There are many who come to the house: tradesmen, servants and visitors.'

'And they would know nothing of this, if you didn't shout it from the eaves,' Helen said, crossly. 'Pray find a more amusing subject to discuss, Mel.' She glanced at Dermot as he took a tray from the room. 'If you want to keep family secrets, you have strange ways of doing it. Every servant now knows that we have valuable books and yet they probably never gave it a thought before you spoke.' Her irritation was enhanced by his earlier treatment of her when he stole her rings.

'The shutters are now secure, Lady Altone,' Jack Vaughn said. 'I keep the keys to the inventory and will soon have a description of each book that would stand firm in a court of law. There is no danger of the books changing hands so long as we have that record, which is proof of possession.'

'But without that proof, the books could change hands freely,' suggested Melville. He sipped his wine and looked thoughtful.

'The whole collection was in a sorry state and no one knew their true value until I made the first inspection. I think the idea of a valuation now is good and I have sent word to a competent judge in London who belongs to one of the major museums. I suggested that he will keep one copy of the valuation in his safe keeping.'

'You have sent?' Melvile said, spilling some wine.

'I sent a groom to catch the mail coach. Mr Lanyon comes here soon and it should be done before he arrives. I still have work to do on the inventory but should have it done before they want to see it.'

The evening became more convivial, with a singer entertaining and bright conversation, but Melville eyed his sister's jewels and said little. She must have a fortune on her neck, he thought. All that wealth and not a thought for her poor brother. The money he had gained by selling her rings had paid his debts and pushed away the danger of a dual, but what now?

Helen showed no sign of tension, and Jack Vaughn marvelled at the change in her from the hard-eyed woman he had glimpsed, to the softly-spoken and charming hostess that she seemed now.

Carriages came to collect the guests from Bath and Melville went into the hall to see them leave. The stout library door was shut and behind it lay the answer to all his troubles. One book, just one of the collection, would pay his way for months, or until Lady Helen had more resources.

If he took one book now, would it be missed? The inventory wasn't complete and no firm copy existed of the record. That damned list! Lights were being doused in the salon and Charmian had gone to her room, pleading a headache. Helen avoided her brother as much as possible and he knew that she would not check on his actions.

He lingered over a last glass of claret and Jack Vaughn went out to the stables to make sure that a horse, badly ridden by Melville, was recovering.

The library was empty. Melville took a candle and slipped inside. He closed the door then lit a lamp on the far side of the room, hidden from the door by a screen. He climbed the steps and took down a book that had not as yet been listed. Was it valuable? Vaughn had said the value varied, and even if the book was old it might not be worth much. He put it back and cursed his own ignorance. Dashed tricky! He took down one book that he knew was in the inventory. It was beautifully illustrated and obviously valuable, but it *was* listed.

He tried the desk drawers but they were locked. The corner of the desk was heavily decorated and he ran a finger along the leaves until he found the spot where he'd seen Jack Vaughn press to release a spring. Inside the tiny opening that clicked free there was a key to the desk. He took it and closed the secret compartment.

He put out the lamp and opened the door slightly. The hall was empty so he walked languidly across to the stairs to his sister's rooms, the key in his pocket. She was sitting at her mirror, dressed in a revealing peignoir. She stared at him.

'And have you some of my jewels that you want to return?' she asked tartly, twisting the rings on her fingers as if she thought he had designs on them too.

'No, sister, I have to leave on private business, making it impossible for me to ride with Charmian and Vaughn.' He shrugged. 'It tires me to be with her and not to have her. That man and her woman watch her from dawn to dawn and I need air.'

Helen smiled coldly. 'I thought it out of character for you to stay so long with a girl as green as Charmian. I have been impressed by your devotion and almost came to believe you loved her, but if you grow restless, it is better to find consolation until you marry.' She looked anxious. 'Be discreet. All is well now, but one hint of infidelity and our little rose will never be a prize in your buttonhole.' She pulled the bell rope and ordered a tisane.

'You have many headaches, madam,' he said. 'Is it a bad conscience or has His Grace looked on sweeter, younger lips?' he said maliciously.

The impotent fury in her eyes amused him, but his smile died as she said, 'Remember, Mel, your popularity with the duke depends on me. If I lose him, then so do you. We have to stay together however much we dislike it.'

Melville went to his room and waited until the house was silent.

Jack Vaughn moved restlessly and then sat by his window, recalling the confusing impression made on him by the household. Lady Altone had so many facets to her nature, and although he couldn't believe that she was really bad, he knew that she and her brother shared a conspiracy that meant to harm Charmian. Of Charmian he dared not think too deeply. He hated the risqué gossip of Helen's friends and wanted to shield the child from their taint. He disapproved of Helen's flowing gowns of exquisite fragility and near transparency when the duke was expectecd to call. Could Charmian ever wear such clothes? The men who would be attracted would desire her but have no respect for her person.

It sickened him to imagine Charmian married to Melville, living with him, being loved by him. It was useless to think of sleep, so he dressed warmly as the late summer was merging with autumn and a chill descended after dark, and he knew that the library fire would now have died.

He picked up his three-cornered hat and decided that a turn in the garden, followed by an hour at work in the library, might bring the elusive sleep. He walked quietly round the house and stopped by the library windows.

A dim light showed through a chink in the shutters. The church clock struck two and by now the household should have been abed for an hour or so. The light brightened suddenly as if a flame was lit and he hurried into the house and went swiftly through the hall. He pushed the library door open and stood aghast. Jack Vaughn clutched the brass candlestick he'd seized in the hall and strode forward.

In the fireplace, the inventory that he had prepared with such care, was fast turning to ashes in the wide grate. Melville held two books in a linen cover and the key to the secret drawer lay on the desk.

Jaspern cursed and turned pale, dropping the books on the desk. He glanced round the room at the weapons that had once graced the long gallery, and caught up a rapier.

Lunging wildly, he flew at the man by the door, but Jack Vaughn parried the thrust with the candlestick, catching Melville on the knuckles and drawing blood. He shouted and a chair overturned, making a loud thud in the stillness. A door opened above, then another and feet hurried along the gallery.

Charmian awoke when Debbie screamed, and Dermot ran down the stairs carrying an old musket. The entire household gathered in the hall.

Melville stood at bay, the sword in his hand. His dressing gown was open at the throat, showing the nightshirt under it, and his mind worked quickly. He held out his bloodstained hand, pointing to Jack Vaughn. '*Murderer*!' he shouted. 'Murderer and thief.'

'No! He is no villain,' Charmian cried. 'What are you saying?'

'I came down because I heard noises in the library,' Melville asserted. 'This rascal was here, burning the inventory, the only record of the books.' He indicated the linen bag. 'Look in there, and I think you might see what he was stealing.'

'But it was *you*! I came in and found *you*.' Vaughn looked confused.

Melville leaned on his sword and smiled. 'And do you dress so completely when you investigate a noise, sir? I do not have time to tie my cravat before confronting a thief. Look at him. He is ready to ride, to take the books to his cronies. I know he went to the stables after you were in bed, so he made a saddled horse ready.'

'You lie, sir,' Jack Vaughn said. He was very pale and sensed the uncertainty of the gathered household.

'Look how guilty he is! I have had my suspicions for a long time and I believe it was he who killed Lord Altone!'

'How can anyone believe that?' Jack Vaughn stepped forward but the servants drew back as if afraid.

'See my hand?' Melville said. 'He attacked me and I seized a blade to defend myself. He killed once and could kill again.'

Several of the servants drew away as if not wanting to be involved. Lady Helen stared at Melville. The *fool*! she thought. He is in deeper than I imagined, but he is my brother and we are caught in the same web. Any scandal concerning him reflects on me. With a brother in prison or worse, what would happen to her?

She could see her future turning barren, with no wealthy friends and no chance of bringing Charmian triumphantly to Bath and the Royal Court and so gaining an enviable position in society for herself. She might even be packed off to Wales or back home to her own family. There was too much to lose, she decided.

Helen gave Jack Vaughn a glance of reluctant compassion. He was very handsome and she had wanted him for herself but now he had eyes only for her stepdaughter. Her face hardened. 'Send for the constable,' she told Dermot. 'Let him decide on the evidence we have here.' She looked coldly at Jack Vaughn as if she had never seen him before ... as if he was a stranger, a thief coming into the house at night. 'If you killed my husband, you shall pay as you will for attacking my brother.'

She tried to look sad. 'How could you steal your mistress's valuables after the kindness shown to you here? It appears that we were all deceived in you, sir.' Her eyes began to gleam with malice. He was better out of the way. She had seen how he looked at Charmian and her own influence with him had gone. What a fool he must be to refuse a bribe that Melville would have offered him if he had remained calm. He could have conveniently forgotten the existence of certain books when the lawyer came again and life would have been tolerable for everyone. What fools men are, she thought.

'I am innocent,' Jack Vaughn said, with dignity.

'It isn't true!' Charmian said passionately. 'You shall not go for the constable, Dermot. This is a terrible mistake and we must talk. Melville, say it isn't true, for my sake.'

'You are too late, Lady Charmian,' Dermot said. 'As soon as he saw the affray, one of the footmen ran to fetch him.' He came closer to Charmian and spoke softly. 'I am convinced that this is a lie, but it will be difficult to prove.' She gasped. 'Listen to

128

me,' Dermot said with more authority than she'd ever heard from her old servant, 'if they take him, I fear he will hang. Her Ladyship has the duke's protection and will care for nothing of justice if she can be kept from scandal.'

'What can we do?' asked Charmian softly, suddenly calm. 'If only my father were here.'

'Have you money and a horse? His own or a gift from you that none may say is stolen?'

Her face glowed and she whispered in his ear. Dermot went unobserved to her room and opened the box that she told him was in the linen press. He took out a heavy leather purse and hid it under his coat, then quickly gathered a few items of clothing from Mr Vaughn's room.

In the hall again, he walked purposefully over to Mr Vaughn and handed him his thick caped travelling coat. 'Come, Mr Vaughn, we must await the Watch.' In a daze, the maligned man followed him and Melville shot a look of triumph at his sister. If the faithful Dermot accepted the explanation, then all was well.

'I'll put him in the shed by the stable, and lock the door, ma'am,' Dermot said, sternly, to Lady Altone. 'Put that coat on, as it's cold in that shed,' he ordered Vaughn.

Outside, Dermot pressed the purse into the man's hand. 'Come now, sir. A present from Lady Charmian. Take her bay mare as a gift. She insists on it and says, God speed. She says you must get in touch with young Mr Dark the lawyer's clerk and a man of good sense. I will send word by mail coach that you may contact him. Keep to the side roads if you wish to avoid highwaymen or any pursuit from here. Lay up by day and ride by night until you reach Chelsea. God keep you, sir.'

'How can I thank you? I know that to remain here would be death and if she believes in me then I must live.'

'If you contact Mr Dark, do not use your name. Say you have news of a button, for I found such a one in the library after the master was killed. It is silver and with an emblem that I do not know. It was none of yours, sir, that I do know. There was a scrap of lace too, and I have it safe until time will tell all. I shall explain to Mr Dark, so go now and take the horse on grass until you leave the spinney. No need to hurry as the constable is a lazy fellow and will take his time to rise from his bed and get here.'

Jack Vaughn clasped his hand. 'Goodbye, my dear friend,' he said emotionally. Dermot slung up the bulky saddle bags he had brought from a side door. Softly, he patted the horse's flank and watched the shadows swallow the fugitive.

Dermot turned to the shed, piled wood and an old settle inside under the window and thrust back the rotting shutters. He firmly locked the door from the outside and scuffed mud under the window. 'Wouldn't keep a goat in,' he said with satisfaction as he walked back to the house.

Charmian looked at him, then looked away, well satisfied by his slight nod. Dermot tossed the key to Melville. 'Best you take charge of this, sir, then he's your responsibility. I want no truck with murder.' He made up the fire and brought refreshments for the family and ordered a good breakfast for the Watch if they arrived in time to partake of it.

'I don't know what to make of you, husband,' Pru said with tears in her eyes. 'Yesterday, Mr Vaughn was an honest man, fit to care for Lady Charmian, good, generous and kind, and a fine man in your reckoning, and today, you find the dampest, rotten old shed to lock him in to wait for those uncouth villains of the law to come and take him and hang him, most like!'

'It's a wife's duty to think as her husband does,' he said calmly.'

'Think as a mad man? Does that make me mad, too? You are cruel and insane if you think the poor soul did any of those things and I'll tell you to your face that you are wicked and mad and no husband of mine!'

He stretched lazily and smiled, looking well pleased.

'Now, what ails you?' Pru demanded. 'You have a crafty look about you. What is it?'

'I did everything you said. I put him in the dampest, rottenest place. It was so rotten, I shouldn't wonder if that shutter gave way. I must look to it, sometime.'

Pru, realizing the plan, flung her arms round her husband and gave Dermot a smacking kiss. As soon as he had breath again, he said, 'Now you know what I have done. I've locked him in and given the key to Mr Jaspern and that's all I've done, or it's all I'm telling you, so wipe that simpering look off your face, my girl, and keep quiet or they'll know summat's up.'

Eight

Jack Vaughn rode until the city of Bath was far behind him and the mare was breathing hard. He slipped from the saddle and rested in a hollow away from the road, blessing Dermot who had stuffed one saddle bag with small clothes and plain cravats and food, and the other with necessities for the horse. Jack rubbed the mare's flanks with rough hessian, removing the flecks of rime and allowing her to cool safely. His exertions eased his own tired limbs and he took stock of his situation. He could pass for a clerk or lawyer on business and he had money to pay his way.

He made for an inn and ate breakfast under the hospitable but curious eyes of the innkeeper's wife. Yes, he was on business early, he agreed. 'No,' he lied. 'No, not London. I go southeast from Melksham to an estate on business.'

He bought bread and cheese and placed the bag of gold safely inside his shirt, pinned to the waistband of his breeches in case of light fingers in one of the alehouses he would visit. He kept only two sovereigns and loose change in his pockets and left the inn with more confidence.

He went west for a while until he found a village tucked away from the road and asked for a room and stabling, pleading a sore foot which would make him delay his journey for a day. 'And landlord, a pen and ink and paper, if you please,' he said.

The day passed peacefully with no hint of pursuit, during which time he wrote to his cousin who was a doctor in Surrey, and to Mr Dark, setting out the events of the previous evening and the fact that Melville was plotting to marry Charmian so that he could control her wealth. He stared out of the window. Writing such things gave him pain but he had to write the truth about Lady Altone shielding her brother and being intent on him marrying Charmian. He reluctantly mentioned that she was having a liason with the Duke of Shalfleet as well.

He made no mention of Charmian's help or what Dermot had done to achieve his freedom, in case the letters fell into the wrong hands. His letter continued:

You may conclude that an innocent man does not run away from justice, but against the duke's patronage I would have no chance.

Mr Lanyon entrusted me with the care of the estates and the well-being of Lady Charmian, and I swear by all I hold dear that I have never betrayed that trust. I fear for her fortune and more, now that I am not there to care for her. Please go to her, Mr Dark. Take control before dishonest hands do harm, and I beg of you, go quickly. I must stay away and am powerless to defend myself, but I know that Lady Charmian trusts me and some of the servants think well of me; Dermot and Prudence, in particular. If you have news for me, send it to the address I enclose and I will call for it in a few days, or write that it must be sent on to wherever I find sanctuary. In this I put myself in your hands that you will not divulge my lodging until I can prove my innocence.

He sealed the letter and gave it to the post boy to give to the next London coach. He then went to look at the mare.

The address he'd given to Mr Dark was of a family servant, now retired to a small cottage in Surrey not far from his cousin's house and where he thought he might hide if necessary. I cannot go directly to stay with my cousin, he thought. The Runners from London would search for me there, but I can go to his surgery as if I am a patient asking for treatment.

He sat by the window with a pewter pot of ale and watched the swifts fly low over the hedges, chasing the gnats in the dusk. He saw pale faces of roses and smelled their scent below him. They were creamy white and delicate, like the roses that Charmian loved ... and hated. How he missed the soft rustle of her skirts as she walked the library, looking at the books and coming to him with any that were interesting. He missed the freshness of her smile and her guileless wonder when he told her of writers and poets and history. He missed the touch of her hand and the sound of her voice.

He shook himself. You are like a lovesick boy, he silently chided. He put down the tankard and sat very still. It was true. He no longer loved her as a sweet child, the daughter of his kind patron. He loved her deeply and passionately as a man loves a woman and he longed to possess her body. He groaned with despair. Would he ever see her again or would he be exiled from everything he knew and loved for ever? The thought of her marrying Melville was intolerable and the idea of another as yet faceless man taking her, was almost as bad. She could never marry a poor fugitive such as he, without a title or wealth.

He heard the evening coach stop in the village on the way to London and wished it Godspeed as it contained his letters. He went to bed and tried to sleep but his dreams were full of dark corners and he woke unrested.

As he sat at a late breakfast the next morning, he heard a carriage stop at the inn. A family stepped out thankfully, and asked for breakfast. Jack remained in his corner, crumbling bread and hardly touching the good home-smoked bacon that lay before him, but he sipped a little mead from time to time. It was becoming more difficult to think of reaching his cousin safely, as he knew that by now the stage coaches would be watched and people along the routes warned about him, but he could not travel exclusively by night. I should have travelled on, he thought, but the horse needed rest as much as he did.

The young boy in the party eyed Jack Vaughn's bacon hungrily.

'Would you like some?' Jack asked.

The boy's father smiled. 'Pray do not trouble yourself, sir. He must wait as we do. Come, George, leave the gentleman in peace. It is impolite to beg!'

Jack Vaughn laughed. 'Young stomachs are empty quickly.' He cut a piece of bacon and placed it on a crust of bread. 'This will help to keep you alive until your own breakfast is ready,' he said.

The father smiled. 'Thank you, sir. We started before dawn to get away early, but outside Bath we thought we were about to be set on by thieves, so after that, we took to the lanes, only to be lost.'

'Thieves? I heard that the Bow Street Runners had frightened away the highwaymen from the turnpike road as the Prince Regent is visiting Bath.'

'They were not thieves in the end, but the constable and his men hunting a murderer who had escaped from a shed where he had been held.'

The boy interrupted. 'They said he had the strength of five men to have broken out of the iron bars that held him,' he said excitedly.

His father shrugged. 'You can see how alarmed we were. My poor wife was quite hysterical. As I had to drive the carriage, she was anxious as we had no guard.'

'If we had been attacked, we would all have been killed! How could they let a man like that escape? They should have shot him at once, or hung him from a tree,' said the gentle-faced wife.

'My dear ... we have only the words of gossip to tell us that the man is a murderer. I asked the beadle and he admitted that he was following instructions but they did not add up to positive proof. There have been too many innocent men losing their lives after too hasty judgements.'

'And would you have us killed in our own coach if we meet this murderer?' she asked.

'I wish I could be a highwayman,' George said wistfully. 'Not to rob,' he said hastily, seeing his mother's face, 'but to have adventures. Do you think we might meet this man, Father? May I ride with you outside and carry the musket?'

'That is enough, George. Allow me to

introduce ourselves. I am the Reverend Silas Brown and this is my good lady, Hermione. George, you know! We are going to Surrey to take a parish there and we have travelled from Honiton over the past few days. This new parish will be of great interest to us. God is good; I have been given preferment and a good school place for George.'

'It will be better for us all,' said Mrs Brown. She smoothed her dark barathea coat. 'I shall be able to have a more interesting social life. We have been buried in a remote village for too long. It is very exciting, Mr ... Mr...?'

Jack looked wildly round the room for inspiration. He saw the polished brasses and the long hunting horn over the wide hearth but they gave him no help. He remembered the whispered instructions that Dermot had given him. 'Mr Button,' he said. 'Mr Button at your service, ma'am.'

'Are you on your way to London?' she asked, noting with approval the well-cut and fashionable coat and good linen.

'I shall go there, eventually, but I go to Surrey first to visit friends. I had planned to leave London until later, but if I find delays on the road, I may change my plans and go there first.'

140

'I pray you, sir, do not go to London. Come with us and protect us!' said Mrs Brown dramatically. 'I know that we shall all be killed if we proceed with no protection.'

'Come, my dear,' her husband said mildly. 'We are in no danger. No more danger than if we had heard nothing about the man the constable is hunting, and we saw nothing untoward. We cannot ask Mr Button to go out of his way to accompany us.' He smiled.

'You must excuse my wife, sir. We have lived for too long in a small quiet place and this is trying for her. It is more likely that we might meet a gentleman of the road than a murderer, my dear, and it would be me who would be killed, as I am driving.'

Mrs Brown cut bread on the wooden board with such ferocity that the crumbs scattered. 'And what would become of us if you were killed? How selfish to leave us alone with a villain who would do, I know not what, with a defenceless woman and child.' She put down the bread knife and dabbed her eyes with a handkerchief. 'I am so upset I know I shall not eat a morsel,' she said, but when the dish of sizzling bacon, fried eggs and potatoes arrived she was persuaded to eat as well as the rest, and even Jack Vaughn recovered his appetite and ate as heartily as his new friends.

It might be of mutual benefit if he travelled with the Reverend Brown, he thought. He could offer protection if footpads appeared and in the event of the constable sending men along the road to London in pursuit of an escaped prisoner, they would be unlikely to take a second glance at a family of two men, a woman and a boy, when they were looking for a desperate man who had fought his way out of stout iron bars ... with the strength of five!

While Mrs Brown rested and the Reverend Brown saw to his horses, Jack Vaughn took George down to the stream to watch the speckled trout, and they fed the fish with pieces of bread. Jack asked few questions, but away from his parents, George wanted to talk about the events of the night.

'We saw a great deal more than Mother knows, as she was sleeping for most of the time,' George said. 'There was one gentleman with breeches over his nightshirt, carrying a pistol. He had one hand bound up and there was blood on it!' he said with relish. 'He was very anxious to catch the man and he called to the men to shoot him and kill him if he was sighted, as he was dangerous, but another man said he must not be shot as it had not been proved that he was guilty.'

George trailed a long grass into the stream and said slowly, 'If I was accused of something I hadn't done, like the time when they said I'd stolen cakes that the boot boy had taken, then I would want to have the chance to explain before being beaten!' He grinned. 'I hope the man they were after *is* guilty and I hope we meet him. I shall hold him off with our musket,' he boasted. He dropped the grass into the stream and watched it drift under the bridge. 'But you *will* come with us, Mr Button?' he asked anxiously. 'Please?'

Jack smiled. Fate was kinder to him than he'd dared hope. Who was he to refuse their protection when they thought he was protecting them? 'Your horses need rest my lad, and so do you, but if we can start early tomorrow, then I will come with you.'

George let out a whoop and ran to tell his father, who embarrassed Jack with protestations of gratitude.

'I believe you have been sent from God, sir. I must hurry to tell my wife of your kindness, as I know it will be a weight off her mind. I shall then repair to the little church and give thanks. I might find the vicar and have time to talk to him,' he added with satisfaction. 'Would you care to accompany me, Mr Button?'

'I have letters to finish,' Jack said hastily, unwilling to sit in a grey vestry while the reverend gentlemen talked of church matters. 'Also, I must ride, to keep the mare in condition for the morning,' he added.

He rode to the hill overlooking the main road from Bath and saw nothing but the golden fields, with the waving heads of grain and the dark green of late summer, touching early autumn; the breeze caught the golden crop in waves of beauty like a burnished sea and he stayed awhile, soothed by the peace. A lone horseman rode below but lacked urgency, and Jack walked the mare back to the stable and left her with a good feed of oats.

George was waiting for him. 'I am bored,' he said. 'I have rested but I can sit no longer. I have been forbidden to wander away and I cannot even go down to the stream alone.'

Jack ruffled the boy's hair. 'Go and ask your mother if I may take you walking before supper. Promise her that you will do *exactly* as I say,' he added with an attempt at a fierce frown. 'And tell her we shall buy fruit for the journey tomorrow from the farm down by the road.'

George came running back, saying that his mother would be very grateful for some fruit. Grateful! thought Jack. If they only knew!

The farmer showed George a foal that was only two days' old and insisted that Jack drank a pot of home-brewed cider before they picked apples and late plums. He left them in the orchard, saying that if they picked a bushel for him, they could take as many as they wanted for themselves. Jack was eager to find an outlet for his surplus energy. He removed his jacket and worked hard, and they filled a bushel basket and then another for the farmer. George selected a huge apple and sat under a tree crunching it, and Jack stretched out beside him.

In the distance he heard horses coming to the farmhouse. The riders stopped for a while then rode off again and Jack Vaughn felt tense, trying to listen to the sounds through George's chatter.

When the horsemen had left, Jack said quietly, 'It's time to go.' George threw away his apple core and helped to carry the apples. The farmer was delighted with the baskets they had picked for him and added a round cheese to their fruit. It was overwhelming, but would he do the same if he knew who was on his farm?

'It's the labour, sir. I can pick only so many and we need the fruit for storing and cider. I could give you both work for a month, young sir, but I think you'll be on your way tomorrow, as I was saying to the constable.'

'The constable?' Jack spoke sharply.

'Why yes, sir. They came and you must have heard the horses? Wanted to know if we had any strangers here or a villain hiding here. Asked if he was in my barn! I said they could look for themselves and if they found a tramp they could see him off for me as I've no time for vagrants.'

'They were looking for tramps?'

'No, sir, it's a proper villain they're after. I told them I had no strangers here except for you and your son, and the Reverend gentleman at the inn.'

'Do you know where they are bound?'

The farmer shrugged. 'I just think they wanted a drop of cider. The heat's off the search and they'll be on their way back to Bath. That rogue's gone clear now, stands to reason. He could be anywhere in any direction from the crossroads.'

On the way back to the inn, George put his hand in Jack's. 'I wish you were my father, as the farmer believed. I love my father,' he said solemnly, 'but he would never pick apples and laugh as you do. May I pretend that you are my father ... or at least an uncle when we travel together? I would like it very much.'

'I'm very glad you feel like that,' Jack said with more truth than the boy could suspect.

After a good meal and an early night's rest, they packed at dawn and a sleepy girl served them breakfast. Jack Vaughn dressed in the cold dim light and put on a fresh cravat. He packed his saddle bags and added fruit and cheese, and a flagon of cider went into the coach with the rest of the fruit, with Mrs Brown and George. The Reverend Brown drove the carriage and Jack rode alongside on the bay mare, carrying the old musket that Mr Brown urged him to take, although Jack suspected that he might be injured more from the back kick of the old gun than any highwayman would suffer from the blast.

Hornbeam Manor seemed far away as if he had entered another world, but he had time to mourn again for Lord Altone, and renew his vow to find who had killed him, to blush over the way he had been deceived by Lady Helen's beauty and to feel the deep love he had for Charmian. Her hair was the bright berries on the hedges and her fragrance was in the autumn tang of woodland and the smell of late roses in cottage gardens.

They made good headway and after two days, Jack Vaughn said a reluctant goodbye to the Brown family as they made for the vicarage in Reigate and he avoided telling them exactly where he would be staying.

At the inn where Jack Vaughn had met the Brown family, a horseman ate a solitary meal and tumbled into bed in the room that Jack had used. It had been a bad day and Melville Jaspern was out of temper. He had searched lanes and villages but had seen nothing of a man alone on a bay mare. He had come back from the crossroads where the others reported no sight of the man and Melville was full of fear that Jack Vaughn was still alive. While that was so, he would have no peace, no security and no certainty that justice could be thwarted. It was important that the matter should not become public knowledge, with important people like the lawyer, Mr Lanyon, protecting Vaughn.

The duke had been explicit. Any scandal linking him to Helen, if she had a brother who had stolen valuable books, and was about steal others, would be intolerable. The duke made no secret of the fact that he thought that Melville had stolen them and waved aside scruples testily. 'Find him and kill him for all our sakes,' he said, and Melville wondered why he was so vehement. It couldn't affect the duke very much. It was common knowledge that he visited Helen, seduced other men's wives and flaunted his victories in the gaming salons. Melville knew him too well to believe that the duke really loved Helen or had an abiding affection for her brother.

He pulled the coverlet over his chest and bent over to put out the candle, then noticed something white on the floor by the bed. He picked it up and examined it, then gave a cry of triumph. It was a cravat, the plain kind that Vaughn wore. He turned it over and saw Pru's neat chainstitch, in red letters, her way of making sure that laundered clothes went to their rightful owners. 'Vaughn' he read.

Nine

Charmian ran to the window to watch the horsemen coming to the door. The man in a tight red coat must be the beadle and the man with two Runners, the constable.

A minute later, a coach arrived and she rushed downstairs to welcome Mr Lanyon and Mr Dark, who had left their coats with Pru as if they had every intention of staying.

'Oh, Mr Lanyon, how good that you are here! Such terrible things have happened and you can have no idea of them.'

He patted her hand. 'We came as fast as we could, my dear.'

'Then you know? But how?'

The lawyer glanced round to make sure they couldn't be overheard. The constable was in the drawing room with Lady Altone and the servants were preparing refreshments for the travellers, so they were alone.

'I received word, but do not ask from whom. A name is not a thing to be used lightly and is best unsaid, is that not so, Mr Dark? But take heart, for I refuse to believe that Mr Vaughn is a thief or a murderer. I think that Mr Jaspern has been a little ... too hasty, eh Dark? Men say things ... very unwisely, things they don't mean, when they are hard-pressed. It is unfortunate.' He regarded her keenly, missing nothing. He saw the doubt and confusion when she was reminded of Melville and his accusations; the man who had been a charming and constant companion, and for whom she had formed an affection bordering on love. He sensed her misery.

'I know that Mr Vaughn is innocent, sir. I could never believe him capable of anything dishonourable. He and I are friends, true friends.' She looked at him with puzzled eyes. 'But if not him then who could have burned the inventory? Who tried to steal the books? The only other person there was Melville and I have affection for him, too.'

He tucked her hand under his arm. 'It is not easy to see when someone of whom we are fond does wrong. It's best to leave it to someone who can judge without bias, my dear. Is her Ladyship at home?'

'She is in the drawing room with the constable and I think Melville is with them,' she said. She drew back from the door.

Mr Lanyon gave Mr Dark a significant glance and pursed his lips. 'I think we must disturb them at once,' he said. 'If you will come with me, Lady Charmian, I think we must see them.'

'Must I? Such matters frighten me.'

'My dear, you are the mistress of this house and you are it's *sole* owner. Now that Mr Vaughn is no longer here to look to your interests, you must take note of what happens on your property and decide what you permit here. Only *you* can decide if Mr Vaughn is accused of theft.

'If no books left the house, there has been no robbery. If he burned the inventory, then you could argue that it was his own work and was not due to be shown to me for another two weeks when he could have had time to make another.' He smiled kindly. 'If you make no accusation, then he is a free man ... on that score at least. Mr Jaspern made another terrible accusation but that is one that must be proved, not based on supposition, before judgement could be passed and there is little evidence to point to the guilty party.' He shook his head. 'Mr

Vaughn was headstrong to run away, but with the mood that Mr Jaspern brought to bear here, the villagers would have strung him up without question ... rough justice, so often misplaced, does happen, eh, Mr Dark?'

He pushed open the drawing-room door and took pleasure in Lady Altone's surprise and discomfiture, and noticed the panic in Melville's eyes. His expression alone was enough to convince Mr Lanyon that here was something needing his attention, and it also removed the last shred of doubt concerning Mr Vaughn's honesty.

'Well, sir, this is a pleasant surprise,' said Helen with a forced smile. 'We expected no visit from you for another week or so.'

'I smelled trouble, Lady Altone,' he said.

'You were told? Who sent word?' Her tone was haughty and hinted at the reckoning she would have when she found who had contacted Mr Lanyon without her knowledge or leave.

'Bad news travels fast, ma'am, but I am glad to say that Lady Charmian has made us feel welcome and has been good enough to invite us to stay.'

The constable looked puzzled. In all his visits, Lady Altone had interviewed him and he had formed the impression that she was the lady of the manor and that Melville, as her brother, was a close advisor and a person of authority.

'I would be obliged if someone would tell me what is developing,' Mr Lanyon said.

The constable stood four square to the window and stood as tall as possible, but only managed to show his pot belly to great disadvantage. 'Lady Charmian? What has a young girl to do with this business? And you, sir... Who are you, intruding into this sad affair?'

The lawyer looked at him sternly. 'Let us make this quite clear. I am the family lawyer and trustee, the sole executor of the will and testament of the late Lord Altone. I have his estates and his daughter in my care, so you must come to me for any information you require, in the absence of Lady Charmian, whose property this is by right of the said testament.' His voice was dry and impressive and the constable was comically deflated. 'Now sir,' Mr Lanyon said briskly, 'having established my authority, have you any objections to telling me of *all* the events as they happened? Or as they are *alleged* to have happened?'

Melville avoided the lawyer's eye and sat

apart as if the proceedings had nothing to do with him. Dermot came in softly with a tray and decanters and Melville filled his own glass as if needing a stimulant. Mr Lanyon held up his glass to the light and smiled. Dermot made sure that when he served the lawyers, he brought only the best vintages.

'You have accusations to make, sir?' Mr Lanyon directed his question at Melville.

The constable coughed. 'It has been established that the man, Vaughn, burned valuable papers and tried to make off with books.'

Mr Lanyon regarded him with disfavour. 'And who established this as fact? Has Miss Charmian accused him? And of what? Of destroying his own work, a rough draft, perhaps? And are any books missing? Have you proof that any have left the house? What titles have been stolen?'

The constable shifted uncomfortably and looked at Melville for help, but he turned away to refill his glass.

'Is everyone here tongue-tied? Did you make this accusation, Lady Charmian?' persisted the lawyer.

'No, of course I did not, Mr Lanyon. I am sure that Mr Vaughn did nothing wrong,' she said with spirit.

'Then what have we? A quarrel between two men in which one had a bloody hand and the other is accused of many acts of which you have no proof?'

'What of the other matter?' They turned to Lady Altone. 'What of my husband? My brother accuses Mr Vaughn of *murder*, not just the destruction of paper!'

'And have you grounds for such an accusation?' The lawyer's voice was intimidating. 'These are grave charges, ma'am. Was it in the heat of the moment, or have you proof, sir?'

Dermot was circulating, handing around sweetmeats. He stood aloof but watched and listened. Why should Mr Jaspern accuse Jack Vaughn? The button did not belong to Mr Jaspern, nor the lace. Dermot had searched his room and there was no coat with such buttons. Perhaps Lady Altone was convinced that her brother had killed Lord Altone and thought she must shield him.

Mr Lanyon had similar thoughts, even when he knew nothing of the button. A pretty pair they are, he thought. Bless my soul, it's high time I took a hand. He glanced at Mr Dark and sensed his sympathetic agreement.

'Well, sir,' he barked. Melville stirred uneasily and shot a glance of pure hatred at her Ladyship. 'Answer me,' Mr Lanyon said. 'Where are all your fine words? Were you hoping for a quiet hanging without trial? A hounding without justice?' He turned to the constable. 'What was said that night after the two men quarrelled?'

'This gentleman shouted that they were to shoot to kill, sir. He said that the fellow was violent and we must raise all the bullies we could muster to sniff him out. I believe that Mr Jaspern went after him with a pistol. All round the villages he went, telling everyone how dangerous the man was.'

'And I nearly had him,' Melville muttered, recalling his fruitless search after he found the cravat. 'I shall get him. I await word from my men who follow a hot trail towards London.'

Mr Lanyon ignored him and said to Charmian, with a smile, 'Tell me, my dear, did Mr Vaughn ever fill you with terror during the many hours you worked together in the library? And more important, did Mr Jaspern give any indication that he suspected the man of murder and that you needed protection?'

Charmian laughed with relief and amusement. 'Mr Vaughn is the gentlest, dearest man.' She faltered and took a step towards Melville. 'Oh, Melville, say that you were angry ... you made a hasty decision. Tell Mr Lanyon that you were mistaken. You know he wouldn't hurt a fly.' She found herself by his side, her face flushed and her eyes filled with tears.

Melville wanted to take the pain from her eyes, but he recalled the threats of his sister and the warning tone of the duke and knew that until someone was convicted of killing Lord Altone, he would have no peace, no ducal patronage and no marriage to Charmian, so he said coldly, 'I have reason to believe that it was he. He has designs on Lady Charmian and her fortune. He is a common fortune hunter and when he knew I was to marry Lady Charmian, he was incensed ... so desperate that he tried to blame me by burning the papers and pretending that no books were stolen.'

There was a deathly silence. Now that the words had been spoken Helen was frightened, but she hid her feelings under an air of hauteur. Mr Lanyon watched and said nothing.

Charmian gasped. 'Mr Vaughn has never made any advances towards me. It is not true, Mr Lanyon.' She looked at Melville, hardly able to believe that this was the man who had held her tenderly and kissed her with such passion, the man who had been an amusing companion and of late had been on good terms with Jack Vaughn. Melville glanced at the shocked faces.

'I should like you to repeat what you have just said,' Mr Lanyon said slowly.

'That I accuse him of murder?'

'No, not that, for I find it too feeble an accusation to take seriously. The other, if you please.'

Melville saw that the shock he caused was from his indiscretion stating that Charmian would marry him. He made an impatient gesture and said, 'La, sir, can I recall every sentence I speak?'

'Allow me to refresh your memory. You mentioned, in passing, that you expect to marry my ward, for that is what she is in law until she is twenty-one. Have I interviewed you with that prospect in mind, sir? Have I? Have I seen this young man with that in view, eh, Mr Dark? Has Lady Charmian announced her intention of marrying him?'

The lawyer saw Charmian's confusion with growing concern. So, the young puppy had worked on her emotions, had he? A pretty kettle of fish, he thought grimly, and one in which I must put a finger. 'I suppose,' he said dryly, 'you had plans similar to those I have heard of ... when young *gentlemen* make up to pretty women with money and persuade them to elope before they come of age? And can you last that long? Have you enough substance to carry you until Lady Charmian is eighteen and inherits the bulk of her estates? Even then, she will be unable to marry or distribute her wealth without my consent until she is twenty-one.'

Charmian heard the lawyer's sarcasm and saw Melville's face. She then knew that this was true, that Melville wanted her for what she could bring to him from her inheritance. She burst into tears and fled from the room.

'Well, sir,' Mr Lanyon said. 'I think you have given the constable reason enough why you wanted Mr Vaughn out of the way, whatever your own guilt might be in the other matters.' He looked at Helen. 'I am puzzled, ma'am. Until today, I believe that you, yourself, encouraged some form of attention from Mr Vaughn, and since the death of your husband have treated him as a friend ... or more. I am curious to know what changed your opinion so suddenly that you now accuse him of a murder of which you know him to be innocent. I suspect that you know more about this sorry business than you admit.'

He strode from the room and told Dermot that he and Mr Dark would require rooms for lodging at the manor.

Helen sank into a chair, her face ashen. It was all going wrong. His Grace was irritable and nothing pleased him. Was he tiring of her? Melville was a fool, and the lawyer had arrived at the wrong moment, before Charmian could be convinced of Jack Vaughn's guilt.

That night, Mr Lanyon and Mr Dark sat in solitary state at dinner. They heard Melville shout at a groom and then the sound of his horse galloping down the drive.

'A sorry situation,' the lawyer said. 'Mr Vaughn was wise to write to you, Mr Dark, and not to me. I can say with truth that he has not contacted me, and you can keep him informed.'

They ate in silence and found the atmosphere of the house oppressive as if waiting for momentous happenings, but when they went to the library, where Dermot had lit a good fire and laid out port and fruit, they were more relaxed among the books and smell of old leather.

Mr Lanyon ran his gaze over the shelves of books, regarding the leather bindings with the appreciation of an expert. He touched one or two and stopped where they leaned slightly at an angle, as if some had been taken and others spread to hide the gap.

'The stupid young puppy!' he said.

'What is it?' asked Mr Dark.

'You were here when the will was read and before that when his Lordship showed us the most valuable of the manuscripts from the monastery. Remember, do you? Know them again would you? Well, Mr Dark, I'd be greatly obliged if you would point them out to me now as I can't see them.'

They searched the shelves and inspected the desk and side tables but the books were missing. 'Only the best for our Mr Jaspern,' the lawyer said. 'Knows a good thing when he sees it, eh, Mr Dark?' He sat back spreading his coat and stretching his legs to the blaze. 'More discrimination than sense,' he said, and chuckled instead of being angry at the way Lady Charmian's property had been treated. 'Make a note, Mr Dark. Suggest that you have business in Bath tomorrow. Say you need to take the waters. Got a touch of gout, have you? Need to visit the spa urgently?'

'But I've never had as much as a twinge, sir.'

'Never mind. Do you good ... vile stuff, but no matter. Cure everything. When you are there, look out for a book or two; something special for a valued client... No name but pay a good price.' Mr Lanyon rubbed his hands together and poured more port. 'Yes, Dark, a trip to Bath will be beneficial. Your client is looking for ancient monastic writings.' His face hardened. 'And when you *do* find them, and you will find them, sir, then send a note by special messenger on a fast horse, and stay with the books, yourself. Find who sold them to the shop and summon the Watch to mount guard so that no message can leave to alert the thief who sold them.'

'But what if they are not to be found?'

Mr Lanyon kicked a blazing log, sending hot embers up the dark chimney. 'Then the sparks will fly with a vengeance, for it will mean they are in a private collection and we shall have to ask awkward questions.' He shook his head. 'This is a dangerous situation but I feel certain that we shall find them in a shop close to Poulteney Bridge as there has been little time to pass them on to a buyer.'

He sat deep in his chair, his eyes half hidden by thick brows. 'I think that our Mr Jaspern will find that all his friends will desert him if he is discovered trying to sell the books. With the murder still unsolved, there will be few takers for the books except to either an unscrupulous dealer who will spirit them away to London or Paris, or a shopkeeper who has heard nothing of what happened here and would buy them in good faith. I think the latter as Jaspern will not know of unlawful dealers and will seek to sell the books as if they are his own.'

'What was that?' said Mr Dark.

Mr Lanyon lowered the wick in the lamp and opened the door a crack. Carriage wheels crunched the gravel and muffled voices came through the shutters. It was very late for a caller and Jaspern had left by horseback and would use the side door, left unlatched for him if he returned late after gambling.

Dermot unbolted the front door and a figure in a dark velvet coat and dazzling lace entered the hall, dressed for a formal banquet and not a private and clandestine visit to a lady. His voice was curt and his face set as the duke ordered Dermot to inform her

Ladyship that he was there. Dermot rushed upstairs to tell Pru to deliver the message as Lady Altone was in her bedchamber, and the tall man in the hall paced like an angry tiger, clenching and unclenching his hands.

As the rustle of Helen's silk peignoir caught his attention, the duke looked up and saw a vision in soft green and lavender. Her hair fell in a golden cascade and in spite of his disturbed thoughts the duke was filled with admiration for the woman who had ensnared him so completely and amused him for so long. He felt an upsurge of desire and went to meet her on the stairs, taking her hands and kissing them.

She smiled slightly, her face strained, her eyes anxious. 'What then, Your Grace?' she asked, glancing below to the empty hall. 'May I offer you refreshments in my boudoir?'

She saw the look in his eyes and was relieved. He still loved her. She would take him to her room and weave the same spell again. How could she doubt his fidelity? He had come to see her, to love her and to tell her that he could not keep away and had risked his reputation appearing at this hour straight from a royal occasion.

Her heart beat faster, but not for joy. He

had come in the *middle* of a royal occasion, from the Assembly Rooms where the Prince Regent sat at tables until the night was old, and it was but one in the morning. The duke dared not flaunt protocol in this manner unless something had happened that was of such great importance that he dared not stay.

'Come, sir,' she said softly and led him to her room. Dermot answered a tap on the front door and Mr Lanyon saw him pointing the way to the kitchens. The duke's coachman laughed and pointed to the stairs, making a lewd remark. Dermot stiffened as he stared at the man under the lamp, splendid in the livery he wore only when he took the duke in full fig to the soirées of the Prince Regent. He wore a fine coat of ruby satin, frogged with black, and over it a three-tiered blue surcoat with silver buttons.

'This is a rum do, Mr Dark. The duke all dolled up to meet the Prince, but visiting a woman late at night?'

'It is common knowledge, sir, that bucks go after young women after the gaming and if they are bored. I've heard that they play at highwaymen and raid farmhouses to take who they fancy,' said Mr Dark with acute disapproval.

'I did not know you could be so loquacious, Mr Dark,' said the lawyer and smiled. 'But then they go masked, in plain coaches, disguised so that they are unrecognized, and never in full dress with a coachman in livery, for all the night owls to see.' He frowned. 'When the duke calls by day, he comes discreetly in the afternoon or with friends for dinner. He travels by plain coach and often on horseback, alone. Very interesting, my dear sir, very interesting.'

They waited in semi-darkness for an hour, until Dermot hurried down to alert the coachman. Lady Altone clung to the bannisters, her hair dishevelled and her robe in disarray, showing the outline of her unbound breasts, still beautiful as a wanton is beautiful, but her eyes were not those of a woman passionately loved. They held fear and desperation.

The duke strode out of the open doorway without a backward glance, and in seconds the night was torn with the echo of wheels and hooves.

Mr Lanyon turned to his assistant. 'Put more logs on the fire. There is still one bird out, and I want to know when he returns.' He called to Dermot who was bolting the door again. 'Mr Dark and I have worked late. Bring us some of that excellent game pie and a stoop of ale, and bring a tankard for yourself. You will not sleep tonight, I wager, and I have things to say.'

They sat eating and drinking as if no barrier of class lay between them.

'Well,' said Mr Lanyon, cutting more pie. 'Where did Mr Jaspern go tonight, I wonder?'

'It's when he returns, I want to know, and I have questions to ask him that can't wait,' Dermot said grimly.

'I know you heard some of what passed in the drawing room and that you are angry, but you must leave all questions to us.' He put out a hand to stop the man from speaking. 'We are all angry and we want to find who killed your master, but there are many fences to clear before we can point a finger, and we must make no mistakes, eh, Mr Dark?'

'Mr Vaughn did not kill my master and, in fairness I think, neither did Mr Jaspern, but Mr Jaspern must not be allowed to marry someone as sweet and innocent as Lady Charmian.'

'We are agreed on that, Dermot. There is no need for you to bloody his nose, get thrown out of the house with no future for you and your comely wife and maybe even see Newgate for your pains.' His eyes twinkled. 'It's good to know you are a man of courage and more honour than many of your betters. Have no fear, he shall not lay a finger on her or her wealth. Mr Dark must remain here until justice is done and Mr Vaughn returns.'

Dermot hesitated then looked into the face of the lawyer and gained confidence. 'I know it was neither of the gentlemen here and I have proof.' He laid on the table two articles: the piece of torn lace and the silver button, and told them where he had found them. 'Tonight, sir, I found out whose coat the button came from. It's the livery worn by the duke's servants. The coachman had such buttons on his surcoat. One of the duke's men killed my master.'

Ten

Melville tapped the tiny enamelled box and elegantly took snuff, brushing the grains from his fingers with a lace-trimmed handkerchief. He watched the tables in the main gaming salon and the purse of gold coins lay heavy under his coat. A good bit of business, he thought. That fellow knew what was good and had not been afraid to take the books.

'I know the gentleman who will want these, sir,' the man said. 'He's a collector of substance and asked me to look out for books of quality.' He'd chuckled. 'He'll be surprised when he sees these as I've never found anything to match them.' He cast a calculating glance at the handsome face, the expensive cut of the suit and the exquisite fall of lace at the throat and wrists and the fashionable languor of the manner. This was no fly-by-night dishonest cove who had filched the books. 'I just want your word that these are your property to sell as you feel inclined,' he said. 'Just a formality in your case, sir,' he added hastily.

'If you have any reservations on that score, I will take them away again. I have no doubt that my patron, the Duke of Shalfleet will relieve me of them, and be reluctant to come to your premises hereafter!' said Melville with more confidence than he felt.

'Oh, no, sir, I apologize if you think I had a moment's doubt.' The man frowned. 'I can pay you only a part of the money now, but if I give you a promissory note for the balance, will you accept it and settle at the end of the month?'

Melville nodded as if the money was of little consequence, but he was almost frightened by the sum the man had offered him. The books were valuable, he knew from Vaughn's assessment, but this sum was far in excess of anything he'd dreamed of receiving. Jack Vaughn must be hunted down and killed long before anyone thought to check the books, as without him, there was no proof that they had existed. Fervently, he hoped that the men he had sent to trail the librarian would find him soon.

The shopkeeper eyed him with interest, thinking that here was a buck from the Prince's entourage who was strapped for money and had probably helped himself to family possessions. He shrugged. That was not his concern. It was a private matter that would not lead to scandal.

Melville bought a leather purse to hang from his waist as there were cutpurses and villains everywhere in Bath now that rich pickings could be made from careless and sometimes drunken men.

Strangely, he was able to view the people at the tables with detachment, with little desire to play. The faces under the glittering chandeliers with the hundreds of wax candles, showed avarice and desperation, triumph and cold ruthlessness. He did not join the party round the Duke of Shalfleet and the brightly dressed ladies who looked towards the duke for favours and excitement, like golden sunflowers turned to the sun.

A lady brushed by him with a rustle of taffeta and the fragrance of roses. It was as if Charmian had passed by, bringing a wave of freshness and calm into the charged and smoky atmosphere.

He took a glass of wine from a silver salver

and sipped it refectively. What nonsense, he thought. I have money to burn and the duke's patronage and the Prince spoke kindly to me and complimented me on the set of my cravat and asked the name of my wig maker. I should be exultant. But inside, he had a heavy burden of guilt and tried to dismiss the faces of his cruel lackeys from his mind. How they would enjoy putting the innocent man to death. He drank more but the wine did nothing to alleviate his dark spirits.

All eyes turned to see the Prince emerge from his private dining room, his intimates hanging on every word. He was ushered to his place at the highest table where vast sums of money often exchanged hands at the fall of a dice. A week ago, Melville would have elbowed his way closer in the hope that the royal eye would notice him, but tonight he held back.

A tall figure in dark velvet stood by the outer doorway, then walked over to the salon where whist was played for low stakes. Melville raised an eyebrow. Shalfleet, coming in late and joining the ladies? He followed the duke. This was interesting. The duke scorned the whist tables and had little time for those with no means to gamble.

Melville looked about him. Perhaps there was a lady there who was usurping Helen's place in the duke's affections and bed.

The duke was not playing but talked to a small group who were obviously flattered at this unwonted attention.

A page boy bowed and spoke to the duke who went into the main salon to greet the Prince, apologizing that he had not heard the arrival of the royal personage as he had been talking to friends in the other salon. The Prince Regent nodded, assured that the duke had been in attendance all the evening and had not insulted his host by leaving the salon.

'Edwin of Shalfleet playing whist? La, sir!' A lady in the royal party put her painted face close to the duke's and tapped his arm coquettishly with her fan. 'Now, sir, tell us the truth. Was it whist or a lady who lured you into such wild entertainment?'

'I assure you, madam, that no lady could persuade me to play whist if I had no desire to do so. I begin to find it a sadly underrated game.'

'Ah, you say that, Your Grace,' she said archly, 'but what of the ladies? You have neglected us of late.'

He smelled the heavy scent from the deep

décolleté of her gown and saw the streaks of white powder on her half exposed breasts. His habitual gallantry made him kiss her hand and flatter her, but his thoughts were far away. This is how Helen will be in a year or two, he thought... When her looks fade and she becomes shrill and importunate. He turned away with a lighthearted quip on his lips and hate in his heart. He saw the raddled faces of women who had lived too hard and the heavy-jowled self-indulgent men. This is a sick and profane society, he thought with surprise at his own revulsion ... and it is my life.

He found a seat away from the tables and was lost in thought. What of his wife and family? He visited the country mansion twice a year but now longed for the smell of earth and his good horses and the simple life. Perhaps he should go there soon. He smiled wryly. They would be shocked if he did so, having left them to their own devices for so long, with the rumours of his excesses reaching them. They would not welcome him.

Melville aproached him and the duke waved him to a chair. They surveyed the room in silence and, to his relief, Melville found that he was not required to talk. The duke stirred and made sure that they were not overheard. 'I paid a visit to your sister tonight,' he said.

'But ... the Prince... Did he not command your presence?' So, that was why the duke had ducked into the small salon!

Shalfleet shrugged. 'There were plenty to take his attention and he has no eyes for any but his new mistress,' he said scathingly. 'He has seen me here, so he thinks I have been here all night.'

'And was my sister well?'

'Troubled!' He gave a cruel smile. 'Much troubled, and I fear that you have not handed Vaughn the ace of spades?'

Melville looked away, his mouth tightening. 'I have the matter in hand, sir. Two of my men are on his trail, with orders to seal his mouth with earth.'

The duke spoke softly with snake-like vehemence. 'He must die soon. Too much time has been wasted.' He beat a ringed hand on the marble table top and Melville stared at the crest on the huge signet ring, the crest that was on all the duke's jewellery, his livery and his carriages; a brand of possession, with power to change a man's fate. But why was it so vital to kill Vaughn? He was a nobody, a person employed to look after books, who the constable believed was a thief and a murderer, so wasn't it safer to let him continue to hide his face and never dare return to Hornbeam Manor?

'You said, Your Grace, that my sister was troubled. Is it about Vaughn?'

'That and other things. I find she grows shrill and tearful and I prefer her as she was, elegant and cool and charming.' It was almost a command. Make her as she was or it could only be a matter of time before the ducal carriage no longer stopped at Hornbeam Manor. The Duke turned a ring on his little finger. 'The other matter is of more concern. If I am implicated, it will go hard with many people.' His face was a mask of evil. 'Many people will wish they had never been born if I am involved,' he hissed.

'But, Your Grace! How could our petty affairs touch you?'

Shalfleet gave a humourless laugh. 'And are you so blind? Then I have hope! If the ones who were there and almost saw the blow struck do not know, then how will others?'

'But you were not there that night. You were here at the theatre, in a closed box to which you had invited me, but I couldn't join you as an angry husband was chasing me over half of Somerset. I arrived home just after the deed, but saw nothing.'

The duke inspected his fingernails and said, 'I think you do not understand the importance of this to me, your sister and to you. This could break us all. It is one thing to dally with the wife of Lord Altone, but another matter to quarrel about it and be implicated in his death, as he was the head of an ancient family. A common farmer can go to the grave unnoticed by the court and society, but a man with such a title causes attention.'

Melville laughed. 'So, one of your men went to avenge an insult from the Noble Lord, and by sad chance killed him? It is simple, My Lord. Bring your rascal to the constable and throw him on their mercy. Society will think well of you and what's one lackey more or less? You can have a slate clean of blame and it would bring the light back to Helen's eyes. It would help me, too, as I needn't kill a man of excellent character whose death would be heavy on my conscience.'

'Many would say I ordered the killing and was covering up by denouncing my servant. It is a risk I am not willing to take. The other solution is best. The librarian must be found and if your bullies have no luck, then *you* must find him. Follow the scent from where you found his cravat. People will tell you more than they'd say to two louts after his blood. Say you are a friend with urgent papers for him and they will talk.'

'Do you know for certain that it was one of your men? Might it not have been as we suspected, a wandering thief?'

'I have reason to suspect that it was one of my household who took it on himself to protect me, out of loyalty to my good name. On the night, you were wenching, your sister was in bed, and I was at the theatre in a closed box with an unnamed lady. My man came home on a nag badly lathered, with a silver button torn from his surcoat. Now, do you see? The button must be found or Vaughn must die.'

Melville let out his breath sharply. He saw the elegant faces of lovely women, heard the brittle but exciting voices and sensed the easy splendour of the Assembly Rooms. All this would be lost to him if his patron was disgraced. He smiled wryly. The duke would loathe being dismissed to his country estate as much as Helen dreaded being sent to the Dower House and the damp Welsh hills.

He thrust away all thoughts of compassion. 'I'll leave tomorrow, Your Grace,' he said. Behind his arrogance, the duke was frightened and Melville felt a surge of power. He could turn the tables and do the demanding now. 'I trust you will find my sister well, *tomorrow* when you call on her, Your Grace,' he said insolently.

Shalfleet gave a reluctant grin. 'I shall owe you a great deal, Jaspern. I shall be pleased to escort your sister to the Assembly Rooms as soon as her period of mourning is over and I shall be pleased to offer homage and hospitality to your future wife when she is presented at court.' He gave a mocking bow. 'Your servant, sir.'

The mention of Charmian on the lips of this reprobate gave Melville an uneasy thrill of alarm. I must keep them apart at all costs, he decided.

Eleven

Mr Lanyon had returned to London, leaving Mr Dark to see to the affairs at Hornbeam Manor, and Charmian rang for breakfast to be served to them both in the morning room. She was cheered by the calm belief of the lawyers that Jack Vaughn was innocent of any crime and she hoped that he would come back soon to work with her in the library. He must return. Her heart beat faster. What would she do if he stayed away? Was it only the bare trees and cold rain outside the window that made her draw her shawl closer against the chill?

She heard a movement, thinking it was Mr Dark, but her smile died when she saw Melville, booted for riding, clad in a heavy great coat, caped like a coachman's. He pulled on thick gauntlets and handed a bag to the stable boy to put in the carriage. He hitched his collar high under the tricorne hat and Charmian had to admit to herself that he was very handsome. His bright-blue eyes gleamed from a smooth unlined face, curiously youthful in spite of the excesses of eating and drinking and debauchery.

He saw Charmian and stopped, the bright colour flooding his cheeks, part-embarrassment and part-pleasure as he saw the picture she made, standing against the deep-ruby drapes, dressed in the warm, long-sleeved dark-green dress. He saw the gold chain at her throat with the miniature of her parents in a locket and knew she needed no other adornment, unlike the beauties who thronged the Assembly Rooms.

'Why out so early, sir? Do you travel far?' she asked coldly.

'I have business for the duke,' he said.

'Do the games never close?'

'Not gambling, ma'am. I ride to find a murderer.' He came closer. 'You are cold towards me but give me credit for this. I am sent by order of the duke to avenge your father.' His eyes held a hint of pleading. 'When justice has been done, will you look on me with more favour?' He swept off his hat and took her hands in his, drawing her near. 'Much of what I said was false, Charmian, but two things are true. I did not kill your father and I love you.'

She saw the agony in his eyes but could give him no consolation. She saw instead the anguished eyes of another man who had never done an evil act in his life.

'I love you,' Melville said again. 'I shall love you for ever.' He saw her displeasure and was angry. He seized her in his arms. 'When I come back, I shall marry you! I can make you love me.' His gloved hand under her chin forced her lips to his.

She struggled free. 'No, sir!' She was half afraid and half thrilled by the masculinity of the man, but her mind told her that here was no future husband, no warm friend. 'You will do no harm to Mr Vaughn?' she begged.

He gave her one furious glance and ran from the house, leaving the autumn leaves drifting in through the doorway. Her concern for Jack Vaughn banished any conscience he had. Her unwilling lips signed the fate of Jack Vaughn.

Charmian shivered in the chill air. Where was he now? Was he well or hounded as a fox is chased by rough hounds?

Mr Dark banished her fears. He was a

good companion who could talk about the estates in Wales and the people there and he was interested in the servants who had come away with Lord Altone, far from their roots to serve him.

'We have loyal servants,' Charmian said. 'They are more. Debbie and Pru and Dermot are my friends.'

'In all the Altone estates, there is a long history of fairness, and good conditions, well-built cottages and extra comforts in times of sickness or bereavement,' Mr Dark said, but frowned.

'And it is so now, even with my father gone,' Charmian insisted, seeing his doubts.

'I agree, and there has never been any laxity of morals,' he said, embarrassed that he might have said too much.

'What do you mean? I thought that all our tenants and landowners set a good example by attending church with their families, and we make good provision for our clergy.'

'Not that, Lady Charmian.' Dermot was mending the fire with fresh logs. He and Mr Dark exchanged glances. 'I mean that women and girls have been safe on the Altone estates,' said Mr Dark and Dermot gave an audible grunt as he bent over the logs.

'What do your know of this, Dermot?'

'Enough,' Dermot said grimly. 'My sister married a smallholder down in Bridgewater and she said that the gentry there are not ... particular. They show no respect for honest womanhood.' He put a log into the depths of the fire and watched it catch alight. 'There's tales of young women being spirited away at night and returning in a bad way, clothes torn, half-demented with fear, and hurt, Lady Charmian, hurt in body and soul in ways I wouldn't treat a dog.'

'Surely the villains pay for their crimes? What says the constable? Have they no magistrates?'

Dermot glanced again at Mr Dark for approval. 'Mostly, it's her word against a great name, and is accepted as high spirits and youthful pranks when it's one of the gentry. Sometimes it's his Lordship himself and there are some who practise outlandish customs that smack of slavery.'

Mr Dark clicked his tongue. 'I do know it to be so, but pray don't trouble Lady Charmian with such matters as I hope it could never happen here.'

'But I must know what happens in other places or how can I ensure that the traditions my father followed might not be lost?'

'There are those who follow the feudal custom of...' Mr Dark coughed. 'On the continent they call it *le droit de seigneur*.'

'The right of the master? What of it? The master has rights and often has his own guard and local laws. He pays well for this honour.'

'This is different. It means that the night before a girl marries, the bride sleeps in the bed of the lord of the manor and he takes her virginity.'

Charmian paled. 'This is monstrous! I have heard of pranks when young bucks seek out village girls to seduce them, but not by force. Debbie told me of one who found a handsome masked lover, who serenaded her and won her, and she went willingly as she thought that under the mask was the man she was to marry. He wore the same clothes but she slept with a stranger!'

Dermot stared. 'I did not know you heard such things, Lady Charmian!'

'It is not strange, gentlemen. Surely everyone has heard tales of the Duke of Shalfleet? He is said to indulge in such matters. Melville told me so. The duke often dresses as one of his lackeys. There was one trip when they were all masked and the duke drove the coach dressed as his coachman.'

She smiled. 'I know it couldn't happen here. Our servants are a part of my family. We walk and talk as friends.' She went to the door. 'Are you ready to ride with me, Mr Dark?'

She ran lightly up the stairs to dress warmly in a thick undergarment and fine velvet habit. In the library, the two men digested what she had said.

'That's it, then, sir. Don't you think that's what happened?'

Mr Dark pursed his lips in the way of a cautious lawyer. 'It would seem so. The evidence points that way and is in character. The duke could come here disguised to see Lord Altone in secret.' He stared at the button in Dermot's hand and then at the lace. 'The button could be from livery but not the lace. Most certainly it was the master, not the man. I must confer with Mr Lanyon.'

He gave Dermot a note to send off, sealed by his own signet ring. 'Watch for Mr Jaspern if he leaves the house. The constable should be here by now to see him about the books, but we must not alarm Lady Charmian until the rascal is taken.'

The crisp air raised the spirits of the two

riders and Charmian found Mr Dark an amusing companion once he'd forgotten to act like a lawyer, and he rode well. They galloped to the end of the chestnut avenue, scattering the fallen leaves and releasing the scents of autumn. At the rise, they stopped to look down at the Bath road. A man drove cows along a muddy pasture and a cock crowed.

Charmian shivered. 'He crows too late. He should have crowed at dawn. Do you believe in evil omens, Mr Dark?'

'For some who have done wrong. The innocent are safe.' He gazed down the road, then back at the house. 'I expected to see Mr Jaspern riding. Have you seen him today?'

'Does it matter? I find your company more agreeable. I think that Melville did take those books. Perhaps *he* believes in ill omens!' She saw his attention was on the road. 'What do you see?'

'Horsemen,' he said with satisfaction. 'The constable and his men. I am afraid that they know who took your father's books, but not about his death.'

'Who do they accuse?' Her face was white. 'Not Mr Vaughn?' She heard her voice whisper his name and knew that she needed to know that he was still at liberty, even if it meant that Melville was guilty. The strong emotions aroused by Melville's passionate kiss could not make her want his welfare as much as she wanted Jack Vaughn to live and to come back to Hornbeam Manor, even though he had said no words of love to her.

'Not Mr Vaughn. Mr Lanyon has proof that Mr Jaspern sold the books to a dealer in Bath. I found them, and have a detailed description of Mr Jaspern as the man who sold them as his own property. There is no doubt now about his guilt.'

'The constable? Is that the reason why he is here?' The high colour in her cheeks showed her distress and confusion. 'Your bird has flown, Mr Dark. He told me he was ordered by the duke to find Mr Vaughn, but it seems that he was running from the law!'

'What do you mean?'

'You should have asked me earlier or the constable should not have been so tardy. Melville took the small carriage and enough clothes for a journey. He told me he was ordered by the duke to catch my father's murderer and he was distraught and in fear.'

Mr Dark turned and rode furiously back to the house, with Charmian close behind him.

In the library, the constable blew out his cheeks and looked important. 'When you saw him gone, why wasn't a search made at once?' he asked.

'I said nothing to the household in case a word or gesture alerted him to your coming. I have never known him leave the park here so early after a night at the tables.' Mr Dark was defensive. 'If your men had come earlier, you would have found him here.'

Rapidly, he regained his confidence. 'If Miss Charmain had not seen you riding towards the manor, she would not have mentioned him.' He dropped his hands to his sides. 'Well, gentlemen, what now? Has he gone to find Mr Vaughn, who we know to be innocent of stealing the books and burning the inventory and I am convinced is innocent of murder, or has Mr Jaspern run to some powerful friend for protection?'

Helen stood in the doorway, cold and aloof. 'He has no patron,' she said. 'After this, no one of rank or birth will look at him. Even his so-called friends of the demi-monde will desert him.' She gave a hollow laugh. 'A patron? How brittle are promises made when all is bright!' She regarded Charmian coldly. 'If your father had given me my rightful place in the estate, I could have given my brother enough to satisfy his needs until he married you.'

'I have never said I would marry him,' Charmian said, with dignity.

'It would have come if others had not interfered. You were not immune to his advances and he has enough charm to convince any woman.' She shot a malevolent glance at Mr Dark.

'I am grieved that Melville has come to this but I could never marry him. Even when he charmed me most, I knew that I wanted more proof of his sincerity and honesty,' countered Charmian.

'Honesty? What has love to do with honesty? My brother has all the charm that has made my family famous. If he willed it, you would want him. Tell me, were you unmoved by his advances even when you mistrusted him?' She turned to Mr Dark. 'Take care, sir, lest she might protect a thief as she tried to protect a murderer. Her tender heart will be her ruin.'

'Mr Vaughn is no murderer.'

'And do you think my brother is capable of that?'

'No ... oh, I am confused. I cannot believe it of either of them but someone *did* kill my father.'

Dermot bent over her with a tisane made by an anxious Debbie. He bent closer. 'Take courage, Lady Charmian, as we think there is another man,' he said gruffly. 'Mr Dark will see it through.'

The constable took his leave, with Mr Dark urging him to search diligently and to make his men understand that Mr Vaughn was to be protected, not hung! 'We have firm proof of his innocence,' he said.

'Proof?' asked Helen.' Is there proof that my brother is guilty?'

'It is not clear-cut, Lady Altone. We believe that there is another involved in this sorry business.'

'I think you are as all lawyers, tying up your words to hint at more than is true. I am not impressed by sober suits and solemn words.'

'I can say no more,' he told her.

Charmian put down her cup. 'If you will leave us, madam, Mr Dark and I have work to do in the library.'

Helen saw a new strength in the girl's demeanour, and to her own surprise, she inclined her head and left the room, walking slowly back to her own apartments. She felt oddly defeated as they knew details of which she knew nothing. Her head ached. A third person? An inexplicable dread filled her heart instead of joy that her brother had so far escaped the arm of the law. Another person? She stared at the pale, drawn face in the mirror and tried to bring more colour back by rubbing her cheeks.

The duke might call. She reached for her tray of cosmetics, concocted by a famous court hairdresser, and began to rouge her cheeks, then dressed with care adding a soft rose-coloured shawl to her blue gown as the cold air penetrated even the firelit warmth of her boudoir. Pru dressed her hair and the effect was good. Helen felt more confident. The fact that Shalfleet had not visited her for a few days was sufficient cause for her depression, but everything would be well. Now that Melville was no longer suspected of murder, anything he would do apart from cheating at cards could be brushed aside as mere peccadilloes.

Even if Melville had stolen books, Shalfleet would laugh at his effrontory and Charmian would never allow him to be arrested for what she considered was a family matter.

The picture of a lovely assured lady was restored and she reclined on a French day-bed, reading a novelette, telling Pru that she was ready to receive visitors.

In less than an hour, the door opened to admit the duke. He paused, then shut the boudoir door firmly behind him. After such a grey morning, and the chill he felt in his heart whenever he wondered if Vaughn would escape and leave the question open as to who killed Lord Altone, the sight of Helen, reclining like some bright Eastern houri, sinuously lovely, scented and beautifully attired, warmed his heart and inflamed his desire. He kissed her hands, then drew her to him and she smoothed the heavy lines round his mouth with a soft finger. He kissed her lips and throat and she exulted in his physical need of her. He was with her and wanted her and couldn't live without her, so she was sure that he must love her.

Mr Dark walked into the yard where the duke's coachman had taken the horses out of the cold wind. He passed the time of day and admired the horses, complimenting the man on the condition of the trappings and admired the colour of the livery. 'This surcoat goes well over the ochre breeches we wear every day and equally well over the formal scarlet livery,' the man said.

'Do you keep your own?'

'Oh, yes, sir. His Grace is fussy about his

livery. Has it tailored as well as his own coats from a good man in London.' He brushed a scrap of straw from his sleeve and slapped the rump of one of the greys. He laughed. 'He likes us to be smarter than any other coachmen, and if he wants to wear the surcoat, he need not be ashamed amongst his friends.'

A prickle of excitement made Mr Dark turn away to hide his expression. 'He drives this coach? I can see that he would need a thick top coat but surely he has many of his own?'

The man tapped the side of his nose and leered. 'There are times when he don't *want* to be His Grace, when he goes after a filly to take his pleasure in secret, if you get my meaning? He's a great man. Takes what he wants and no questions dare be asked.'

'Surely a man of his standing wouldn't confide in you?'

'Lord, no, sir, I know my place, but it's understood that he does take the coach. I find my coat with mud and creases and once with a button missing that had to be replaced in a great hurry. He was put out, I can tell you. It had to be sewn on again before the house was awake.' He gave a coarse laugh. 'That must have been a rough night!'

Mr Dark nodded to Dermot, who was standing back but heard every word. A witness now, he thought, but even more need to keep their own counsel or this poor wretch would be in danger from the duke. As he went back to the hall, Mr Dark saw Prudence hurrying to the boudoir with refreshments. Charmian was in the study, completely engrossed, and Mr Dark silently thanked heaven that the duke had no designs on her. He shut the library door firmly and sighed. It was easier to deal with dull documents than to act as nursemaid to a lovely heiress.

Lady Helen handed a glass of French wine to her lover now that passion was spent. She watched him drink and experienced revulsion at his appetite for food and wine and sexual satisfaction. In her heart, she knew that he lacked any real respect for her and she would never hold his love if he desired other women, but for now he was in a good mood.

'Did your brother leave early, madam? I sent him to find the rogue who killed your husband.' His eyes were half-closed, his face expressionless.

'He left very early, sir.'

He grunted with satisfaction but noted that she turned the rings on her fingers nervously.

'You are disturbed about him?'

'No, but the lawyer staying here seems to see everything.'

'What does he say?'

'He says that neither my brother nor Mr Vaughn killed Lord Altone.'

'Zounds! The Devil take him!'

'I am worried that Melville has gone to kill an innocent man. If he kills Vaughn, that will be murder and he will have to flee the country.'

'You need not worry, my dear. Leave everything to your brother. He knows that my patronage depends on this matter and he must do my bidding.' His smile was cruel.

'They talked of a third party. What of that?'

'What indeed, madam. What indeed.'

He pulled on his coat and kissed her hands. Helen went with him down to the hall and he paused to look out of the window to see that the coach was ready.

The door of the library opened and as the duke went out to the coach he carried with him the vision of two women; Helen in her rich clothes, her regal woman-of-the-world bearing and her face rouged and powdered above the low cut revealing gown, and the girl with soft eyes, a simple gown over a gently curving figure with a slim and lithe unrestricted waist. She had stared for a moment like a startled fawn and vanished into the library again, a beautiful and entirely desirable wraith.

Twelve

Mr Lanyon buttoned his greatcoat high under his chin. He put the letter he had received from Mr Dark in his pocket and called for the carriage. It wasn't far to Reigate, but he anticipated the bumpy ride with a lack of enthusiasm. The country roads would be filthy with mud, fallen leaves and the dung from hundreds of horses on the road from London to Epsom and Guildford and the Surrey Downs.

There was no help for it and the messages that he'd seen from Mr Dark needed attention. It would at least be pleasant to take good news and put an honest man's mind at rest. He gave the coachman the address of Dr Vaughn and hoped that his cousin Jack was hiding somewhere close by.

Mr Lanyon checked to see that his flask of spirits was full. 'Never travel without it,' he said to his clerk. 'A mouthful of spirits keeps up a man's own!' His clerk smiled weakly at the dour humour.

The cobbles rang under the horses' feet and the wheels sent up a spray of mud to those unfortunates who walked on the narrow pavements, even if they wore pattens, the thick, heavy, wooden overshoes ringed with metal, that kept them free of the worst of the mud.

Mr Lanyon bought a handful of hot chestnuts to warm his hands as the carriage swept out of Vauxhall and towards Surrey. He was impatient. If Jaspern was carrying out the duke's orders then Jack Vaughn could still be in danger unless his killing was prevented, as the duke had much to lose.

They passed the turnpike and Mr Lanyon told the toll keeper to keep a lookout for a fair-haired man of arrogant bearing, in a small carriage. 'Mark him well if he asks the way, but do nothing to stop him. Tell the Watch to follow him. He is wanted for felony and could be dangerous.'

It was a relief to know that the carriage had not passed the turnpike and when he arrived at the doctor's house he was greeted with warmth, and the insistence that the lawyer should look on the house as his home for as long as he required it, rather than having to stay at the Red Lion.

'We have much to thank you for, sir,' the doctor said and sent word that the lawyer had arrived, to the cottage where Jack Vaughn was staying, and by nine o'clock they were eating roast mutton and drinking a wine that even Mr Lanyon found palatable.

'I thank you, sir, for coming all this way to set my mind at rest,' said Vaughn. 'But what of Lady Charmian? I have grave doubts ... I fear that she may entertain a great affection for Mr Jaspern and will be hurt whatever the outcome of this sorry affair. Is it possible to cease to care for someone even if he has done wrong?' He stood up to go back to his lodging. 'If he hurts her in any way, in body or spirit, he will answer to me. I pray that the constable will catch Jaspern before he regains her sympathy.'

Mr Lanyon regarded the young man from under heavy brows. Now there's a thing! He's in love with the girl. Poor man; he has no land, no title, no wealth and no hope of winning her. He looked about the comfortable but simple room. Nothing to be had from this place, except for honesty, goodness of heart and kindliness. He sighed. Not a bad inheritance for all that, but not acceptable as an entré into society.

'Take good care, Mr Vaughn,' he said. 'Stay firmly in the saddle. You have a few more hurdles to clear. I shall call on you tomorrow before I leave.'

Jack Vaughn walked to the top of the hill at the edge of the town and watched the ragged clouds washing the moon's face, hiding her brightness and then giving glimpses of the sleeping town. The waving branches were like those by the rose garden at Hornbeam Manor, where Charmian had clung to him after refusing the roses he'd picked for her, the rose called Moonlight, that had shed its petals over her dead father's face.

He could almost feel the softness of her breast when he had held her close, smell the fragrance of her young body. He shook himself. Did she smile at everyone as she did with him? It would be easy to think that she had a special feeling for him, but he had seen her in the arms of Melville Jaspern.

He looked down to the road, attracted by a sound. He saw a horse being ridden slowly as if tired, and on his back was a tall man in a smart riding coat. In the fitful moonlight, the white buckskin breeches gleamed and the boots reflected the light. Jack Vaughn stood close to a bush and peered through the darkness until the moon escaped a cloud and briefly showed the man's face.

Melville Jaspern, tired and dispirited, rode on towards the inn and the inn keeper came out to point the way to the doctor's house. Melville seemed to come to life and rode towards the square, with Jack Vaughn following, wondering how he could alert his cousin and acutely aware of his own lack of defence. Melville, on the other hand, was well armed with a pistol and a sword carried from the saddle.

The horseman drew rein at the house and dismounted. He pulled a velvet mask from his pocket and with his face hidden he walked softly to the door, then called in a loud voice, 'Jack Vaughn! Come out. I know you are there. Come and face your fate!'

A chink of light appeared at an upper window as someone peeped out. The shutter moved and the light widened. Jaspern raised his arm and aimed at the window, the firearm cocked and ready to fire. In horror, Jack Vaughn shouted to the person inside, and then showed his face for long enough for Melville to recognize him. He turned away from the assassin as Melville Jaspern swung his arm and fired.

In the stillness of the sleeping town, the noise was as loud as thunder. Candles flickered in windows and legs were thrust into breeches, women cowered under bedclothes and dogs barked. Jack Vaughn lay still, crushing wet leaves, with blood seeping from his side.

Jaspern thrust the gun away and grabbed the bridle of his frightened horse, then spurred him for speed until the beast's flanks were bloody. He raced behind the hill and was out of sight before the first of the townsmen was mounted to follow.

The Watch came with lanterns. 'Highwayman! It must have been a highwayman. I saw his mask,' one man said, and among the confusion Dr Vaughn bent over the still form of his cousin and called for a wattle to carry him inside.

Mr Lanyon was full of horror and remorse, knowing that the young man had saved his life at the risk of his own! Through the shutter he had seen Melville take aim at the light he had so carelessly made visible, and heard Jack's warning cry which turned the gun away, and then... He closed his eyes, shaking with unaccustomed emotion. He couldn't recall a time when he had been so concerned for a fellow human being. 'Only the best, sir ... the very best. See he lacks nothing, spare no expense if he lives. Saved my life, damn it! Only the best, eh, sir? Pray God he survives. Never forgive myself.'

Horsemen spread across the Downs but Melville had doubled back to Redhill as he knew his nag was almost exhausted. He thought with longing of the fast phaeton he'd left while he took a fresh horse, to give the greys time to rest. He found a dry cave by a gravel pit with water for the horse and he wrapped himself in his coat and settled to rest.

If I get clear, he exulted, I shall have everything. They'll never prove I killed him and the duke will protect me. Soon, I'll marry Charmian and I can sell what I like and nobody can tell me what to do!

The Duke of Shalfleet sat at table, feeling an irrational and unfamilar ennui. It was too early in the evening for much excitement and his companions were dull. He glanced at the ladies and saw the same jaded faces and coquettish smiles and heard the same brittle laughter. The Prince had left for Brighton and another lady, and his entourage had gone with him. None of the women left in the Assembly Rooms made Shalfleet want an affair. He thought of Helen and cursed. Why was she still in mourning for her husband? She should be there to amuse him and play cards with him and be available for dalliance behind the curtained alcoves in the gambling halls.

These woman are cattle, he decided. Large hands and strident voices and they wore their beauty patches as if they concealed small pox! Devil take them and Devil take the Prince ... and Melville. Where was Jaspern? How soon could he be sure that the death of Lord Altone was accounted for in the killing of Vaughn?

The French wine was smooth and Shalfleet drank deeply. He refused to pit his wits against these yokels and longed for Helen's supple white body and small smooth hands. He called for his coach and walked carefully, finding the way uneven and the lights blurred.

His coachman grinned. His Grace had had a bellyful! Shalfleet saw the grin and struck the man in the face with his glove. 'Take your insolence off, damn you! Give me your coat. I ride alone.'

A footman and the coachman watched

him leave. Shortly, the coachman ordered a fast horse and borrowed a surcoat and followed at a distance, so that the duke would be observed but unaware of the fact. The coach travelled slowly, then as the driver gained confidence and his head cleared, the horses were whipped and the pace quickened.

'Helen! I'll go to Helen masked and she'll think I'm an abductor until I am lying with her, and then she will have no doubts!'

He whipped the horse again. Where was Melville? He might be back at home with Helen. It was three days since he left to find Vaughn and must by now have news of him. Seeing Melville would be an excuse for visiting the manor so late and he had to know. The last time he'd driven alone he'd lost a silver button that might lie between his safety and disgrace. Once Vaughn was dead, they could produce as many silver buttons as they liked for all the good it would do for justice.

He stopped behind the manor and he tried the door that Melville used. It opened readily and he pulled a mask from his pocket and went in slowly. In the woods an owl hooted, screeching down on its prey. The duke listened. A door opened and he drew back into the shadows. Soft footsteps in the library and the glow of a lamp showed a woman there. A servant? Helen? No, not Helen as she had told him she would never go into the library alone at night.

His Grace smiled, his face a mask of cruelty. A servant? Perhaps the pretty wife of the man Dermot? Perhaps tonight Helen could sleep on and he would take a different pleasure. Who would know? A mask and darkness and her word against his? Frightened and struggling he would take her out on to a bed of moss.

A breeze from the open door pushed the library door further open and he saw a figure against the window drapes. Shalfleet stood still. It was not Prudence and it was not Helen. He was filled with forboding. It was a girl dressed in outdoor clothes.

Charmian had been walking in the garden as she was sleepless. He hesitated. Charmian bore a proud name and was no easy prey for the aristocracy. She was no wanton and she was a virgin.

The wine still urged him to action. A virgin fit for a duke. It would be madness, a small inner voice said, but the wine dulled all but his desire. Charmian bent over the desk, folding a letter ready for sealing. She had written to Mr Lanyon and was still wide-awake.

She turned and opened her mouth to scream but a hand in a leather glove stifled her cry and a face stinking of wine was close to hers, the eyes glinting madly through the black velvet mask. She saw the cuff of a dark blue coat and silver buttons.

The distorted voice that hissed, 'Be quiet!' was the voice she'd heard the night her father was killed and she knew that this masked man was his murderer. 'Not a sound or you die,' he said roughly.

She gave one look of terror and swooned. The heavy folio on the desk slipped and thudded on the floor.

'Who is there?' asked a voice from the gallery. The duke carried her quickly to the coach and turned the horses, whipping them into a gallop. The coachman followed, glad that his master hadn't stayed for hours as the night was now cold.

He followed the duke to a small farmhouse that was used as a guest house for the Shalfleet cronies when the Prince was in Bath. There was a housekeeper and two servants who kept the place ready for immediate occupation and they knew better than to query anything that occurred there.

The Duke stopped and shouted to wake the servants, cursing the delay. Charmian moaned and stirred and he took off his mask and the coachman's surcoat. The fumes of wine were wearing off, leaving a sensation of unease. His courage vanished and he looked down at the girl with sudden panic. What had he done? Even his rank would not protect him if he raped the daughter of the late earl. I'll have to wait, he thought. If I take her, it must appear to be with her consent.

The housekeeper came, looking shocked and frightened when she recognized Charmian. I've seen enough, she thought. I've turned a blind eye to many things but this must not happen.

Shalfleet carried Charmian into the house and laid her on a couch. 'Come, Nancy,' he said. 'What think you? Do not stare at me so. I found her wandering and when she saw me, she swooned. That cursed coat makes me look like a highwayman.'

When Charmian awoke, he was sitting taking snuff and was dressed in the elegant suit of dark velvet he had worn to the Rooms. There was no sign of the blue surcoat or the mask.

He smiled politely, kindly. 'Good, you are

recovered. I fear that you were distracted with fear, my child, but if you wander alone at night you must expect to be scared. I brought you here for your own safety but what your stepmother will say in the morning when she finds that you are not in your room, I cannot bear to think on't.'

'But, I ... the man in the mask?' She stared at Nancy. 'He wore a mask and had a blue coat. It was in the library. I saw but his eyes, but heard him speak and I know that he was the man who murdered my father.'

Shalfleet raised a sardonic eyebrow. 'Give her laudanum, Nancy, and put her to bed on a truckle in your own room. I shall take her home in the morning, unless she needs a physician for a fever of the brain?'

Nancy gave a sigh of relief. 'I'll take care of the young lady, Your Grace. Come, my dear, no one will harm you if Nancy is here.' She gave the girl a draught of laudanum and sat in a rocking chair until Charmian was asleep. She only half-believed the duke. Obviously, the girl had been frightened, but by whom? Nancy closed her eyes as she rocked. 'Please God, it isn't true.' Can the duke have added murder to his sins?

She went down to the kitchen to make a soothing posset for herself. Shalfleet was sitting at the table with a carving knife, sawing away at the thread holding the silver buttons of the blue surcoat. 'What are you doing, sir?'

He put the last button in his pocket and tossed the coat to her. 'Get rid of it. Give it to the first tramp you see if you can't bring yourself to destroy it.' He noticed her pallor. 'Come, woman,' he said testily. 'Have the night's events turned your brain? Think you that I am responsible for this girl and her wanderings? She has been strange since her father died, giving way to odd fancies that every shadow holds her father's murderer.' He looked at the coat. 'As for that, I tire of my livery and find it dull against the Prince's colours. Over the buff uniform, I think a deep violet or a dark green with orange revers and a special surcoat of black to wear over the Court scarlet.' His tone was bantering as if the greatest problem in the world was the choice between violet or green.

Nancy relaxed. The gentry had more money than sense. Only he would change an entire livery for a whim. She managed to smile. If he said it was so and no harm done, she must believe him. She put hot embers in a warming pan and warmed his bed sheets before she went back to Charmian and her own room.

The duke undressed, thinking morosely that this was not the end he had planned for the night, a bed warmed by the dying embers of a fire and not by the hot passions of rape. He dreamed of horses and death and thought he heard voices below. In the morning, he was too preoccupied and tired to wonder why his coachman had spent the night at the farm and the coat had gone.

He ordered the coachman to ride to Bath and give a note with details of the new livery to a tailor. 'Order another coat. Your's came to grief last night,' he added. 'This time, no silver but bronze buttons, as silver tarnishes too readily in the damp.'

Nancy handed the coachman a heavy bag, containing the coat. Without livery buttons it would make a good smart coat for when he was away from the duke's service. She fingered the one button she'd cut from the lining, a spare in case a button was lost, but she couldn't find another. Usually there would be two spare ones, but perhaps one had been used. Silver was valuable and she knew where she could sell it, but she put it in a pewter mug on the dresser and forgot it.

Charmian woke with a headache. The

drug had made her sleep heavily. Nancy brought breakfast to the bedroom and, slowly, the events of the night came back. Had she been taken from the house by her father's murderer after she swooned? The duke said he found her wandering in a distressed state. Had she escaped and been rescued by the duke, a man who filled her with revulsion in spite of his charming and elegant manners?

She dressed ready to go home. The duke kissed her hand. 'I hope you have dreamed away your fears, my dear. I shall trust nobody but myself to take you home. I have sent word to your stepmother to tell her where you are, so there is no need to hurry. Tell me,' he said casually, 'what do you recall from last night?'

'I find it hard to think of last night, sir. I recall walking because I couldn't sleep. I went through the orangery and down by the rose garden, then returned and wrote a letter.' Her eyes grew large with fear. 'A man, masked and in a dark coat, seized me and I knew no more. I felt that I knew him but could not remember where I'd seen him.'

The duke murmured sympathy. 'Poor child. It was fortunate indeed that I was passing. I must have frightened the brute away. You were dazed and wandering. You remember nothing of his face?'

'He was masked with black velvet and his face was half-hidden by the tall collar.'

The duke put away his snuff box. 'You are safe now and we must ride. Although I told Helen of your return, I have to see a friend on the way, a few miles off the road to Hornbeam Manor, but you will not mind waiting for me?' She looked uneasy. 'Am I not to have the reward of your company as I rescued you last night? I find riding through woodland tedious.' He sounded as if he were offering a sweet to a small child to gain favour.

'I will come with you with pleasure,' Charmian said politely.

Nancy told them that Lady Altone had received the message and wanted them to hurry back as she expected good news from London.

'Then we must both hear her good news,' the duke said urbanely.

He handed Charmian into the coach and tucked a fur rug round her knees then put on the bright surcoat he'd worn to the Assembly Rooms and left in the coach once he'd changed into the livery. The horses trotted under the groping fingers of bare trees and Shalfleet let them idle as he thought of Charmian as he'd seen her that morning, with her eyes still heavy with sleep and her hair tousled, lacking the good hairbrushes of her boudoir and Pru's skilled hands. It gave her a look at variance with her usual calm and ordered demeanour. It was the look of a girl ripe for love, a sweet almost gypsy disarray. He thought of her soft full lips which hinted at unawakened passion and the gentle roundness of her thigh as he tucked the rug close to her.

It would be madness! It could lead to his utter ruin, but he desired her more than he'd wanted any woman. He needed to crush her in his arms, to make her responsive to his caresses and to strip her body and possess her utterly, body and soul.

He turned the horses at the fork in the woodland track away from Hornbeam Manor, away from safety and convention and the fact that his rank would not protect him if he raped the earl's daughter.

Charmian lay back among the cushions, her eyes heavy and her mind still blurred by the drug, and she fell asleep.

Thirteen

Dr Vaughn stood by the bed and allowed his hands to tremble and his face to look drawn for the first time since his cousin had been carried inside with a bullet from Melville Jaspern's gun in his body. The lead was out and the bleeding plugged, but he was as yet uncertain of the man's fate.

Mr Lanyon led Dr Vaughn to a chair and made him drink wine. 'You have done everything humanly possible for the boy,' he said. 'The rest is in God's hands. Most distressing for you to operate on a kinsman.'

Mr Lanyon looked at the man on the bed. The boy almost gave his life for me, he thought. He's close to death and that shot was meant for me. He gave the doctor more wine and tried to talk to take their minds away from the near tragedy.

'Is Mr Vaughn a first cousin?' he asked.

'As you can see, he's many years younger than me and is the son of the second wife of the baron who died two years ago. His mother died in childbirth and the baron married again a year later, making three marriages in all. The present baron was the only son of the first marriage and Jack took but a poor share of the estate. There was no other issue. I am only a second cousin but we have loved Jack since he was a child and tried to make sure he had a home here when he needed it.'

'It seems hard,' said Mr Lanyon. 'He is a man of breeding, good looks and has an excellent character, but his future is unstable if he wishes to join society.'

'He was content until now.' The doctor hesitated. 'He confided to me that he cannot return to Hornbeam Manor even with his name cleared as he has fallen in love with the heiress there.'

'I see.' The lawyer put his fingers together in an arch. 'His mother and her family were not rich?'

'There was property and a noble title, sir, but the line had no male heir and the lands went to the Crown, instead of his mother. I do not understand such matters.'

'Where was the estate?'

'The land was in Scotland and the title vested there, too.'

The lawyer stood up and paced the room. 'It might be worth a visit to those estates to check what happened to them.'

'I doubt if Jack could afford your services, sir.'

'You say that to me!' said Mr Lanyon in a low emotional voice. 'He saved my life and I owe him an undying debt. If there is anything there, I will find it. In Scottish law, inheritance can come from a female line.'

Mrs Vaughn was quietly tucking in the bedclothes and removing all signs of blood. Miraculously, the room was homely once more. She moistened the pale lips and passed aromatic salts under Jack's nostrils, but the man lay still.

By next day, Mr Lanyon was rested and full of good resolutions. He sent men to scour the countryside for Jaspern with orders to kill if he showed resistence. The carriage was found at the livery stables where he had left it and taken a fresh nag. With only one now tired horse, he can't get far, Mr Lanyon thought grimly. He must make for friends or the shelter of a patron and he might not be aware that the Runners had been sent after him for the theft of the books.

More important was Charmian's safety, as Mr Lanyon could imagine that Helen and Melville, with the duke's help, would put pressure on her to marry and so obtain control of her wealth. He arranged for all roads to be watched and even the packet boats at the main ports to France and Ireland.

On the third day, Jack Vaughn opened his eyes and smiled recognition at Anne, Dr Vaughn's wife. He ate a little porridge and beef tea and they knew that he would live.

News came from all quarters as the hunt spread and many innocent travellers were accosted and made to prove that they were not murderers, but Melville Jaspern was oblivious of the chase although he went with caution in case his name was linked to one smoking pistol and a shot in the night. He took his time, eating in remote inns and drinking from streams while his horse cropped grass, but one night he felt uneasy and stayed by a stream instead of finding a lodging. He thought of the comfort of Hornbeam Manor but it was worth a trifling spell of discomfort if he was to know that one day he would have his heart's desire. He saw Charmian's face in his dreams and day dreams and knew that his love for her was sincere.

By the time he reached Melksham, he felt safe and started early on the last leg of his journey home. The morning was bright but cold and he walked the horse on grass until the surface frost of the lanes had melted.

A horse whinneyed and he heard carriage wheels. Melville rode over towards the sounds and saw a coach with a girl in the back, asleep. He didn't look at the coachman as such minions were beneath his notice. The driver was having difficulty with the lead horse that had dragged the traces as he slipped on the icy path. The beast reared and the coachman dismounted to calm him and Melville dismounted and tied his own horse to a tree.

As he turned, Melville saw his face and gasped, recognizing the girl, the coach and Shalfleet in place of his coachman. For a moment Melville was delighted, thinking that his patron had heard of Vaughn's death and had come to meet him, but he saw that Charmian was in a drugged sleep from the laudanum that the duke had slipped into her breakfast chocolate.

Jaspern had been a party to many of the duke's escapades, but this was different.

Shalfleet and Charmian? He was stealing the gentle virgin that Melville wanted to marry! This practised lecher was taking her to deflower as lightheartedly as he would take any village jade!

'*Shalfleet!*' His horror and, by now, implacable loathing rang in his voice, like a pistol shot on the frosty air. The duke was still pulling on the bridle of the sweating horse, but he turned his head. 'What are you doing with Lady Charmian?'

The duke saw the cold fury in the younger man's eyes and stepped back. 'I saved her from a masked assailant, my dear boy,' he said. 'She will tell you.' He stopped, knowing that they shared the same memory, of a farmer's daughter abducted after drugging her, and returning her soiled and ashamed after two days with the duke.

Shalfleet saw that there was no explanation that would satisfy the furious man. 'Devil take you,' he said carelessly. 'I mean her no harm. See, she sits alone, coming of her own free will. She had a bad experience last night and Nancy took her into her own room and gave her soothing syrup, but I swear she stepped into this coach of her own free will.' His hands grew moist, his mouth dry as he watched the man raise the muzzle of the gun that had shot Jack Vaughn, but he affected indifference. He turned away to the horse again, knowing that Melville would not shoot him in the back, as he was, after all, of the bon ton, a gentleman.

'Tell me of your progress,' he said calmly, once more the dominant master, and Melville's gun wavered. 'I am eager for news of Vaughn. Did you use that toy on him?' Melville put the gun in his belt.

True, Charmian didn't look dishevelled, but could she have been drugged before being placed in the coach? With no sign of a struggle from her bed? He saw the victorious gleam in the duke's eyes and raised the gun again.

'*No*! You die if you so much as scrape my skin,' the duke shouted. 'Think man!' he rasped. 'You are confronting a noble duke, a close friend of the Prince Regent. I have enough influence to hound you and your sister off the face of the earth.' He watched Melville's face. 'Yes, your sister! She is the cause of all this. She knows I killed her husband.' He gave a short laugh. 'Did you ever doubt it? I killed him to avoid one scandal and you must not think I would do no more. I can ruin you both and remain unscathed, but if you fire at me in anger, with no seconds to give you honourable discharge, then I may die, but you will die on the gallows as a creature too low to be dispatched by a bullet or sword. Have you no sense of honour? This is a matter beyond lust for one simpering girl. Do we fight as gentlemen or be friends? Come now, winner takes all.'

Melville felt an unwilling admiration for the animal force of the man. A duel would give them an equal chance, with honour, and if he killed the duke, it would not lead to the gallows as murder would do. 'We have no seconds, sir. Only the lady and workers from the fields.'

Shalfleet laughed, eager for the wager with death. 'They shall serve.' He called the bemused yokels and stationed one at each end of the clearing. Charmian stirred but did not open her eyes.

'My challenge, your choice of weapons,' said Melville, his own excitement growing. It was better so.

'I have no love of lead,' said the duke. 'Swords will give more sport. I have them in a locker and we may have sport that does not end in death. Agreed?'

'Say three hits with a blood letting?' Melville's pulse raced, and Charmian woke to a sound of swords clashing as they had done in her waking dream. It became the same nightmare of reality she had on the night her father was killed. She pressed her face to the window and saw two men, divested of their coats, circling each other in silk waistcoats and white buckskin breeches. She saw the slender grace of Melville, the man who professed to love her but who she knew to be false and wished to rob her, and she saw the dark powerfully built duke, with his strong shapely legs dancing with elegance as the two men thrust and parried, each seeking an opening.

Nothing made sense! Why was she in a carriage in a clearing of woodland, watching the Duke of Shalfleet and Melville fighting with swords? The sun-raised moisture hung above the woods in a hazy bar, so it was early and she knew she was away from Hornbeam Manor. She tried to tell the men to stop but she seemed to have no power in her voice. 'I must think,' she murmured and tried to regain her composure and to remember the events of the past day and night.

Of course, the duke was taking her home, but this was a wood far from Hornbeam Manor. And Melville? How was it that he was here? He had said he loved her. Hastily she checked her clothes and found she was fully clothed and no attempt had been made to violate her. She blushed to think of what could have happened alone with either of them, in her drugged state.

They fought on, the naked blades glinting with cruel intent. The Duke lunged and Melville's sleeve glowed red. 'Pinked, Devil take you!' he said, ignoring the sharpness of the thrust and the trickle of blood, then pressed forward and the duke had to retreat against a hedge of thorns. To avoid them, he stepped badly and Melville slit his buckskins from knee to waist. Shalfleet put a hand over his wound briefly then recovered and circled again.

Charmian came to the conclusion that they were fighting over her. The duke had abducted her but how had Melville known? Or was it a ploy to get her alone in the wood and now they had fallen out and fought for ... possession? She thought of Jack Vaughn and her heart was heavy. Even now, he might be lying dead in another glade of the wood as she knew that Melville would hunt for him relentlessly. If he dies, how can I face life without him? She now sensed that whoever won this contest would come after her to claim the prize, and she did not relish being alone with either of them in their present mood of elation and lust. A remote wood with two scared labourers as chaperones! It was no place for a girl who valued her liberty and her virtue.

She crept up to the coachman's seat and gentled the horses. She watched the contest which had developed from a formal duel into a fight for life and death. Shalfleet was limping and the blood from a gash over Melville's eye forced him to brush away the blood impatiently. He breathed hard. Another wound and he would lose the contest and Charmian would suffer. His agony for her safety made him cunning. He lunged and broke short, sidestepping so that the duke followed through to the place where he had been, and left his side unguarded. With a single graceful movement, Melville's sword went home and the duke sank to his knees, his life's blood following the withdrawal of the blade. He grimaced in agony and dropped his weapon. 'Devil take you and that whore your sister.'

Charmian saw one labourer run to the distant farm for help and Melville panted and was dazed with victory. He looked up and saw Charmian and the unholy joy of triumph over a powerful adversary gave him the feeling that he could do anything. He would take his prize and no one could deny him! She was his alone and for ever.

Charmian saw the bloodlust and the breaking of his moral fibre as he tossed aside his sword and made for her carriage. She caught the reins and turned the horses to go back the way they must have come and so find a road to safety. She heard the shouts of her thwarted lover, then silence, the blessed silence of the open road as the icy breeze caught her hair and the hooves rang with a song of freedom.

I have watched a man killed and yet I am strangely happy, she thought. Her head cleared in the air. The duke was dead, and from his unguarded voice, she knew he was the one who had killed her dear father.

Melville was far away, with no horse... Or was he? If he had not been with the duke then he had a mount. At the top of rise she listened but no pursuing sound came. It was cold and she remembered the thick fur rug in the coach so she stopped to bring it to wrap round her legs on the open seat.

She urged the horses on and in the distance she heard hoof beats gaining on her. Even if it were Melville, he was far away and the farm drew closer and she felt safe. She passed the plumes of smoke that showed where charcoal burners lit their fires and went on along an old Roman road, long and straight and level enough to make a lone horseman confident. She stood to make the horses go faster, as she had seen her father do, calling them any names that came to mind. 'On, Sheba! Come up, Satan, run on, Sarah!'

The farm lay ahead and Melville lashed his mount in fury, the gap becoming less with every second, but Charmian knew with a feeling of relief that she would be safe in just another minute.

The rug flapped now that it was insecure, and she pushed it away from her feet where it was in the way. It slid over to one side and slipped again as the carriage went downhill, its heavy edge hanging over the back of the near horse. Charmian saw it disappearing and reached down to catch it, releasing her grip on the leather, and the horses were confused. They lost their rhythm and there was a rending snap as one of the iron links in the springing parted when the thick rug caught in the wheel. The carriage slewed to an untidy stop, barely fifty feet from the farm gates, shuddered and one wheel sank into the ditch.

Mellville was a few hundred yards away and coming fast downhill. She struggled to the ground and bundled her skirts indecorously round her waist and ran to the farm, the blood in her throat hot and her breathing painful. Her clothes were heavier with each step. The smoke from the farm chimney was peaceful and hinted at warm family life with deep inglenooks and bacon hanging from ceiling hooks, but the windows were empty and no one saw the exhausted girl.

Melville gave a whoop of triumph as he caught up with her as she clung to the five-barred gate. For a full minute, they leaned against the wooden bars, too exhausted to move or speak. The stain on Melville's sleeve had spread and his face was pale under the splashes of blood on his head. She saw that he needed a surgeon.

Melville saw the wildly heaving bosom and her flushed face and his heart lost its triumph. She was more lovely than even he remembered and her fear would have added spice to his lust, but he was now cold and weak and his desire died, leaving only the wonder of her beauty and his love for her. He wanted only that she would touch him and smile at him again.

Charmian saw the dulling eyes and her fear vanished. 'You are sorely hurt, sir!' she said as he fell in a deep faint. She opened the gate and ran to the farmhouse, calling for spirits and linen and a litter on which to carry him, and when she sat by his couch, she had tears in her eyes. She had seen the unfeigned devotion in his eyes as he fell and her heart was touched. He was a rake and a felon and what was left for him? He had fought for her but he would never possess her.

Later, the redcoats came and stood by the bed, alerted by the farm workers who witnessed the duel. 'He is too ill to move,' Charmian said.

'He is wanted for murder, ma'am, or near murder.'

'But this was a duel. They fought as gentlemen and I saw it.'

'No, ma'am, not that. The duke is dead but this is another matter. A man lies close to death with a bullet wound. This happened in Reigate and if that man dies, it will be murder in cold blood against a man carrying no weapon. This man will hang,' he added with satisfaction. He turned away from the bed. 'I await instructions, so he can stay here and you may give him any attention you think fit, ma'am,' he said kindly.

Charmian sent for the local doctor who cleaned his wounds and stopped the bleeding and she gave Melville sips of wine and gruel when he opened his eyes and could hardly believe that she sat by his couch. By evening he was much recovered but weak, and Charmian promised to stay at the farm until morning when the soldiers would come for him. She was sad. Melville was a villain and Jack Vaughn was close to death. What waste, she thought. What a lonely place Hornbeam Manor will be with no gaiety and no Jack Vaughn to care for me, to ride with me, to be with me.

She looked at the pale face. Melville had been kind to her in many ways and made life amusing, but she could never forgive him if Jack Vaughn died. His charm remained and she knew that she would always feel a kind of affection for him.

The duke's abandoned carriage waited, with the horses warm in the farm stable, ready to take her home the next day, and the soldiers nodded by the fire, exhausted after a long hard ride to reach the farm and knowing that their prisoner was too weak to escape.

The farmer's wife gave the soldiers strong ale and good food and made a strengthening broth for the prisoner, and when he looked at her, she thought that she'd never seen such a handsome man and couldn't believe that he had done the evil things that were said about him. A young man as beautiful as he was must be good, she decided and her pulse beat faster each time she touched him.

The house slept and the farmer's wife listened to the snores of the soldiers as they lay by the hearth. Even the lady was asleep in the tiny room at the side of the kitchen. The farmer was away in a distant pasture with a cow due for calving and the only ones awake were the prisoner and herself. She got up softly and took him brandy and saw the blue eyes glinting in the firelight. He whispered to her and she helped him outside to the privy and waited for him in the darkness. He was much stronger now.

A faint whinny came to him and he saw the white apron of the farmer's wife, like a moth in the night. She handed him a heavy smock and he recoiled from the smell that no gentleman would endure, but she insisted that he slip it over his head. Already he wore the heavy corduroy breeches that the farmer had lent him instead of the tight buckskins. They were loose and comfortable, if inelegant. He stared at her with growing joy. She was offering him one chance of escape. It was a chance he must take even if it risked a bullet in his neck. If Jack Vaughn died, his only future lay on the gallows. He seized the woman with a low cry of joy and kissed her firmly, with a return of bold and dashing gallantry. She smiled, her eyes misted as she pointed to the lane where the duke's carriage waited, the horses hitched and restless to be off.

'Make for the Dover packet,' she said. 'Have you money?' He nodded and embraced her again. 'I put your saddle bags from the other horse, and food and cider in the carriage,' she said and helped him to climb the stage, leading the horses until he had the reins.

'Goodbye, my love,' he said, softly. 'I shall never forget you.' At that moment he could not tell which woman fitted that description, but the farmer's wife stood with her handkerchief to her face, knowing that she would never forget him or this moment in her dreary life.

When the carriage had disappeared into

the night with barely a sigh from a brushed leaf, she returned to the warm farmhouse, the tumbled couch and the snoring soldiers. She went to her own bed and dreamed of a handsome man who smelled of pomade and whose lips were soft and passionate. He said he'd never forget her.

Melville rode hard, safe in the knowledge that the hunt for him was off now that he was captured and lay wounded in a farm.

He smiled. It was worth the risk of recapture, just to smell the night air and have freedom to move, a freedom he would relish long after the charms of any woman had faded. If he lived, his mistress would be freedom.

Fourteen

News had come that Melville had been taken and that Charmian was safe. Pru rushed down to meet her young mistress and Dermot took charge of the redcoats who had escorted her home. Lady Altone stayed in her rooms, unsure of her own future but ordered Dermot to find out what had happened when Charmian was abducted. Her unease was mixed with cold fury and she hated her former lover and Melville, equally.

Charmian told her story, and said at last, to make the women smile again, 'So, my dears, I am back with you, unsullied and complete as I shall ever be.' She added regretfully, 'The duke is dead and Melville escaped last night, taking the duke's carriage, and I have no news as to Mr Vaughn and if he is to recover.'

'Dermot sent a man to find out, Lady Charmian,' Pru said. 'I believe he is still alive but at death's door.'

'What happened when Mr Jaspern was found to be gone?' Debbie asked.

A hint of a wicked smile touched her lips as Charmian explained. 'The soldiers were asleep, confident that Melville couldn't go farther than the privy in the yard and each one thought the other was on watch. They snored after drinking the farmer's strong ale and when they woke, they thought that Melville was in the yard as his buckskins were still by the bed with his jacket. One of the soldiers suggested that they ought to hide the breeches in case he made a run for freedom but the other laughed. They put on their uniforms and ate some bread with ale and one went to the privy and found it empty. I dressed quickly when I heard shouting and the farmer came in from the barn where he'd been since first light and was surprised to find the redcoats there as the duke's carriage and horses had disappeared. The farmer's wife was even more sleepy than I was.'

She looked at the enthralled faces and seemed pensive. 'He must be very strong,' she said. 'No one heard him take the horses and put harness on them and it takes an effort to hitch horses to a carriage, with one arm wounded. The farmer was more concerned at the loss of his muddy breeches and a smock that was missing, than the fact that he had escaped. I slipped him some money to buy more and he calmed down.'

She paused to drink the rapidly cooling tisane and Deb could hardly contain her impatience. 'What then, Lady Charmian?'

'The soldiers rode off to search for the carriage, but found no trace of it and couldn't be sure which road he followed as the men had been told that the hunt for Melville was over.'

'I know it is wicked to say so, but I hope that Mr Jaspern escapes. I wouldn't want a fine gentleman like him to be hanged or sent to the hulks to rot with all the cut purses in England.' Pru blushed. 'He had such a way with him when he wanted something.' She put a hand to the cheek that Melville had once kissed. 'He is a fascinating rascal.'

Charmian smiled sadly, remembering that charm and the expression of genuine love she'd seen as she tended him at the farm. Had the farmer's wife been immune to his charm? How could a man as weak as he was, harness horses and climb unaided to the stage? How did he find the smock in the dark? She had given the woman money, gravely saying it was for her trouble and for the food that the soldiers had eaten, but they had exchanged glances and smiled as both knew that the money was far too much for such trifles.

'Have you word of Mr Vaughn?' asked Prudence.

Charmian looked sad. 'Melville confessed that he shot him and although he might not be dead, he thought the wound would be mortal. He did it on the duke's orders as he was afraid of losing his patronage and he half-believed that Mr Vaughn had killed my father, but the duke admitted to him that it was his sword that killed him.'

Debbie fussed about her. 'Never mind, my lamb, you will forget about this and next year you will find dozens of gentlemen eager for your company at court.'

'I want nothing of court! I want to go back to Wales where there is no violence, no envy and no attempts on a maiden's virtue. But I shall take happy memories of Mr Vaughn who has been a true friend.'

'He may live. We must hope and pray and when Mr Lanyon comes here in a day or so, he will tell us more.'

Mr Dark sent his respects and asked her to meet him in the library as soon as she was rested. She hurried down at once.

'First, may I congratulate you on your escape,' he said.

'I am well, sir,' she said impatiently. 'Have you news from Reigate?'

'Only that Mr Vaughn was shot, as you know.'

'Melville confessed to me that he had shot and killed my dear friend,' she said, her voice trembling.

He looked surprised. 'But Mr Vaughn lives. I have a letter from Mr Lanyon, sent by fast courier. He lies ill in his cousin's house but he sends his humble regards to you.'

'He lives?' For her the room seemed full of sunlight and she wanted to shout her joy. Mr Dark envied the man who could make a lovely girl so happy, then she recovered and spoke primly. 'I am glad. He has been a trusted friend.' The words were inadequate but what could she say? He was a trusted friend and servant of the manor, but one who had believed that Lady Altone was a woman without flaw. I wonder if he still loves her, she wondered. 'I beg your pardon, Mr Dark. I was overcome and didn't hear you.'

He told her the gist of the letter that Mr Lanyon had sent and how Jack Vaughn had drawn the assassin's bullet away from the lawyer and taken it himself. He told of the days when the man lay unconscious and how he needed a long time to recover.

Charmian told of her abduction and about the blue surcoat with silver buttons on the masked man, and Mr Dark called Dermot to show her the button he had in his possession. 'It is the same,' she said and recounted what Melville had said, that the duke had killed her father while wearing the coachman's livery, as he did when he went about his amorous adventures.

'A clean sword thrust was too good for him,' Dermot said.

'It's good to be back among my friends,' she said tearfully.

A swish of silk and they realized that Helen had been listening. She went away to the orangery, her fury of the past few days giving way to genuine grief. She fingered the magnificent jewel that the duke had given her and consoled herself by believing that she had won the love of a very powerful man. No other woman had replaced her.

She turned away from the bleak scene

beyond the windows. What good was his patronage now? Her brother had gone, never to return if he had any sense, and he had killed Shalfleet. She blessed the fact that it had been in an honourable duel or it would leave a stain on her. The future lacked colour and hope.

Mr Dark coughed and she started. She regarded him coldly. He was the minion of that terrible lawyer who had hounded Melville over the stolen books. She turned to him haughtily. 'I give you leave to disturb me, sir, even though I refuse all callers. I am not in the mood for idle gossip, and I have heard most of what has happened. I believe none of it, but that is my concern. I am not involved in any crime and am sad at the loss of a friend.'

Mr Dark listened and turned away but paused by the door. 'Mr Lanyon follows hard on his letter and will wish to see you, ma'am.' He gave her a keen glance. 'He will want assurances of your good will towards Lady Charmian and your promise to keep to your part in bringing her out for presentation at court.'

She glared. 'It seems, sir, that my stepdaughter has won all hearts. She does not say, however, that if it was not for her sly ways, laying traps for my unfortunate brother, he would not have been led into evil ways or killed a man for her sake. He would be here, giving his support and protection.'

'You may think that, ma'am, but Mr Lanyon has decided views and proof to the contrary. He says in my letter that he will want to talk to you seriously. If you now feel that you are unable to fulfill your obligations to Miss Charmian, and to do so in good faith, then he sugests that you leave for the Dower House in Wales immediately.' He smiled kindly. 'I tell you this now so that you may ponder and decide before he arrives.' He hesitated. 'If you will pardon me, ma'am, it would be a waste ... a sin for a lady of your accomplishments to hide herself in the country.'

Helen extended her hand and he kissed it. As he left, she was looking chastened and thoughtful. He was right. She had much to lose. She must wipe out all her association with the duke, not cling to it as a sign of past greatness. All would be well! She was still officially in mourning and had never appeared in public with the duke and his dissolute cronies. In public, she was the grieving widow.

She pulled the bell rope to summon Prudence. 'Take your mistress my best love,' she said. 'Say that I am at her service. I will not trouble her until she wishes it, but remind her that I am waiting to continue our lessons for her coming of age celebrations.'

Mr Dark saw Pru hurry up the stairs with the message, and he grinned. Mr Lanyon had made no reference to Helen in the letter, but surely it was better for Lady Charmian to have the woman as a friend than an enemy? She would know all the wiles of fortune hunters and charlatans and smell them out at the first meeting. What better protection could there be? Set a thief to catch a thief, he thought.

On the night packet from Dover, a man leaned against the wooden rail and watched the wind take the sails. The lights from the shore dipped through the trees and the beacon on the hill burned bright. The sky was clearing and the tarred ropes slid from the moorings. He felt an almost physical pain of a broken bond. He was leaving his whole life and he knew he would never see Charmian again. She would never forgive him and he dared not return. This was a clean break, sharp and final. He was reminded of a couplet he'd heard in Bath:

My soul, like to a ship in a black storm,
Is driven, I know not whither.

As the gap between ship and shore widened, his spirits rose. He was safe and he was *free*. He had money in plenty until he found some source of revenue, as he'd found a fat purse of gold among the clothes that the duke had in his carriage and he had the money from the sale of the books. He also had the duke's thick surcoat, and some clothes which he found in a small portmanteau, together with a jewel box containing some valuable pieces. One ornate ring bore the Shalfleet crest, enough to give him entré into any of the smaller continental courts. He glanced at the other figures by the rail and noticed a fresh looking face gazing at the shore, her skin white in the moonlight. He edged nearer and smiled, with enough warmth to inspire confidence but with restraint as if to indicate that he knew she was a lady.

The girl smiled shyly and glanced up at her father who was staring back at the land. Melville sauntered to the other side of the man and commented on the weather, and soon they were in conversation. Melville chose to ignore the girl until her father turned and introduced her as Caroline, his daughter, half-British, half-French and on her way to visit a relative in Lucerne.

A handsome French lady appeared and noted the good looks and bearing of the young man. She asked many searching questions to which he replied in a muted voice that he had few plans other than to visit Switzerland. How odd that they were going on a similar route. Could he offer them a comfortable journey in a carriage he intended ordering as soon as the ship docked? He apologized for keeping his coat closely buttoned while they ate, but he had a small wound which was more comfortable so.

Caroline's eyes widened. 'It is a mere scratch,' he said. 'Acquired in a duel. Yes,' he admitted reluctantly, 'I was protecting a lady's honour and the man has been dispatched.' He looked forlorn. 'I came to Europe to allow tempers to simmer down and to escape the bullies employed by the man's family.' He turned sad eyes to Caroline. 'I have no friends, not a soul on this side of the Channel to whom I may go.' He brought out the ring with the Shalfleet crest. 'I have only this, a gift from my patron, a noble duke.'

'Then he can help you!'

'Alas no, he is dead, but it may give me some introduction into society.' He paced the deck, alone, his shoulder low as if it gave him much pain, and the new friends regarded him with compassion.

'*Le pauvre ... si gentil, si brave*,' Caroline said and the soft young eyes already held the dawn of love.

In his cabin, Melville tossed all the papers which held a reference to his identity from the porthole and watched them float away and sink. He was now Sir Melville Hornbeam, in a new birth. He kissed his hand to the unwinking moon and said farewell to Charmian. The continent might be exciting, and maybe it was time he married and settled down.

Fifteen

Mr Dark took Mr Lanyon into the library as soon as he arrived, where there was a good fire and a tray of tea and muffins waiting. He told him of the interview with Lady Altone and her reaction.

'You should have been in the Diplomatic, eh, Dark? But you did well. I distrust that woman but I think now she knows which side her bread's buttered.'

Charmian ran into the room. 'What news, sir? Is Mr Vaughn recovered? I have thought of him... As he was of such help to me and I am naturally concerned for his welfare... As I am for you, sir, and hope you are well.'

'He is very low, ma'am. Very low.'

'How is it that you frown? Has he relapsed and is worse? He should be here where we can nurse him back to health.'

The evidence of her concern in the tumult

of her bosom and the blush that appeared when she mentioned his name, made Mr Lanyon satisfied, but he remained solemn. 'I fear that it will be many weeks before he can return here to see you, as he must stay in his brother's house and then visit his cousin again.'

'His brother? I don't understand. His brother had the title and the estates and showed no concern for Mr Vaughn!'

'Half-brother, ma'am. It is true that there is no love there but Mr Vaughn needed to search for papers that have nothing to do with that estate and are his by right of birth, as they belonged to the lady who was his mother, but was not the mother of his half-brother.'

'If he can work there, he should come here, where I need him!'

'He might as well be there, ma'am. He feels useless. He can no longer carry out the duties for which Lord Altone employed him here, and I am afraid he will remain low until he finds a worthy occupation that gives him pleasure and fills his time.' He smiled. 'Someone must fill his place here until he is fully recovered and you may want to have a permanent change to rid you of unhappy memories.'

'That is not so, sir.'

'But you need a librarian.'

'I can do that work until he is recovered. Please, sir, I will hear no more of this. How can I dispense with his services when I look on him as a dear friend?'

'The estates must have a secretary. You cannot take on that duty as you need all your time to prepare you for your coming of age.'

'Fi on that!' She stamped her foot. 'I do not care for Bath or London or the stupid people who frequent gaming salons.'

'You must come out as your father wished,' he said sternly. 'There will be many young men of rank who will want to meet you and to court you, Charmian.'

'I shall not marry.'

'Even so, there is still the problem of someone to look after the estates. I think that Mr Vaughn may have other plans and have taken on other responsibilities that will leave Hornbeam Manor without a secretary.'

'He would leave me thus?' Her face was pale. 'This is his home, so pray tell him so and to return as soon as possible.'

'If you could write to him, it might have more impact than the verbal message brought by an old man. I want what is best for him as he has done me a great service and I owe him my life.' He blew his nose loudly and told her a highly-coloured version of his escape when Jack Vaughn took the bullet that would have killed the lawyer, and Charmian listened fascinated and close to tears.

Mr Lanyon consented to Mr Dark remaining at the manor until Mr Vaughn returned or a new secretary could be found, and Charmian had to be contented with that. They went to dress for dinner and when they were at table, Mr Vaughn was not mentioned. Mr Lanyon regarded Lady Altone with interest. He could never trust her completely so it would be as well if Dark stayed for a while, but he marvelled at her composure. All traces of grief and anger had gone, leaving her face delicately sad and appealing. Her perfumed hands were eloquent as she described her plans for Charmian's court presentation, as if nothing had happened to put off the schooling.

'We shall need an extra dressmaker,' she asserted. 'Charmian must be the best-dressed girl in the county as befits her position and her prospects.' Mr Lanyon nodded approval, and she was encouraged to show off her knowledge of court behaviour and the bon ton of the courtiers. She mentioned what etiquette must be mastered if Charmian was not to appear like a gauche country girl.

In spite of her mixed feelings for Melville and the death of her lover, Helen was determined not to lose her position and so was prepared to do all she could for her stepdaughter, and Charmian gradually forgot the ache in her heart whenever she thought of Mr Vaughn. She responded to the magnetism of the older woman as her charm was as potent as Melville's and her best weapon. Helen listened to suggestions made by the lawyer and added her own. Mr Lanyon was well satisfied. She knew what she was about and, with Mr Dark there as security, she could not be negligent or too extravagant. He sighed with relief as he could now get back to matters that interested him and leave the trivia to Helen and Mr Dark.

Charmian waved him goodbye the next day with many messages for Mr Vaughn and she sent a note, scribbled in haste, sending her kindest thoughts and begging him to come to the manor at the earliest opportunity. She promised to write again at length, but the dressmaker came and the wig maker and Helen whisked her off for fittings and shopping and lessons in deportment, leaving little time for writing.

The house was alive again. The servants rejoiced to see Charmian's renewed interest in all the things a young lady of quality should be finding amusing, and a procession of seamstresses and dressmakers and dancing instructors came and went, each contributing to the polish and finesse that Helen demanded. She was a hard taskmaster but found to her own surprise that she was enjoying it all. There was power in ordering and supervising every stage of the training, and pleasure and pride in the results of her care.

Helen began to wonder, as this was such a pleasant way of life, if it might be preferable to looking for another husband or lover. There were many girls needing her skills and she had the added advantage of knowing a lot of people in the social scene.

Charmian stood before the cheval mirror while Debbie fitted padding to her hips. She eyed it with distaste. 'I shall appear deformed,' she said. 'I am not that shape and I feel clumsy.'

Debbie and Pru were shocked. 'But all great ladies wear padding,' Pru said and

Helen nodded. The figure before her took shape, abandoning the free fluid lines of the pretty girl for the more stylishly fashionable silhouette demanded by high society. It no longer mattered to Helen that Charmian was beautiful. With the duke dead, she no longer feared her as a rival and she pulled her décolletage even lower, making Charmian blush and swear she couldn't appear in public dressed so. Her pretty bosom was almost completely exposed and thrust upwards by stays. Dress after dress was fitted, poems in velvet and satin and lace, with fine silks from China that rustled softly over the many petticoats. Others in soft fine muslin clung to her shapely limbs in the Greek tradition, which Helen said must be worn damp to cling even more. It was a passing fashion but one that Helen thought would show off youth and innocence with subtle allure.

She grew critical of hair and face and throat and concocted lotions of elderflower and rosemary, egg whites and powdered orris, even rubbing the girl's hands with a cream in which arsenic was mixed to give the skin whiteness. Silk stockings came from Italy with satin slippers and shining pumps of calf; head dresses to hold flowers were constructed by the wig makers.

Helen taught Charmian the art of flirtation with elaborate fans of feathers and Pru experimented with beauty patches, placing one close to the mouth or the eyes to discover the most flattering position to draw attention to her best features.

Charmian was like a child with a new toy, absorbed in her role and the days passed by without even a short note passing to the man who had nearly died. When she thought of Mr Vaughn, it was with resentment that he had not returned to Hornbeam Manor. If he could travel to his brother's castle, he could have come to see her, but sometimes when she lay in bed, tired but unable to sleep, she thought of his strong arms, his fine mouth and the warmth she had felt when he was by her side.

She would write tomorrow, but she felt strangely shy, unwilling to show how much she wanted to see him. It was nearing the time for her debut, so the letter didn't get written.

Mr Dark gave her news of him and she tried not to show her chagrin. It was clear that he had forgotten her. He was now in Harrogate, taking the waters. If he needed a spa then why not Bath which was conveniently close to the manor ... and the girl who remembered him with an ache in her heart?

'And after Harrogate, Mr Dark?'

'Baden, I believe, Miss Charmian. Mr Lanyon insists that he does not return until he is really cured.'

'Please wish him well when you write.' she said coldly. 'I have no time at present, but I shall be pleased to see him if he comes to Hornbeam Manor.'

She went to her room and decided that she had to write to him. He was still a friend and she had neglected him. She told him of the preparation for her debut and enquired about his health. She gave the letter to Mr Dark to put with the post but he said he doubted if it would reach him as he had left on the Dover packet.

'Why does he not come here?' she burst out. 'Are we not dear friends?'

'I think he may not feel like that,' Mr Dark said. 'I do not believe he will come, as he has had no word from you except a formal note and he may not write unless you invite him to do so.'

Charmian gave a brittle laugh. 'That is ridiculous. We are friends. He knows he may write to me.'

'I think not,' he said firmly. 'He is a servant of the manor. He is a valued one but still in the employ of the estate and must never presume on the familiarity that you suggest. He has nothing in the way of business to discuss at present and so no cause to write.' He spoke gently, seeing her concern. 'You are about to become a great lady, Lady Charmian. You will notice the difference in the approach of your friends and acquaintances when you take your position in court circles, and now that Lady Altone has heard that Lord Saxom, who is sponsoring you, is certain that you will be offered the position of Lady of the Queen's bedchamber, or some such high office, the difference will be even more marked. Unsolicited correspondence will be an imposition,' he added.

Charmian tugged at a lock of hair nervously. 'But I shall never wish my real friends to treat me any differently because of protocol.' Her hand picked at the edge of her shawl like a hurt child, bereft of the veneer of sophistication. 'Do you think he stays away because he thinks I have no need of him?'

'He has gone away to take the waters and to plan his life. He has no title or wealth.' The young laywer looked slightly puzzled.

'Mr Lanyon has not discussed his situation in detail, but I think that he is to make Mr Vaughn his heir as a gesture of gratitude. There was talk of him going to Scotland after Baden, so perhaps he hopes to manage an estate there.'

'Scotland now, sir! He seems to enjoy better health and fortitude for travel than I could ever have. If he's well enough for that, I need him here!' She stamped her foot, and looked really annoyed.

'He may not feel welcome, knowing you to be fond of Mr Jaspern, the man who tried to kill him.'

'Oh, I have been stupid. Tell him that I know Mr Jaspern to be an evil man who did much harm. I shall never forgive him for what he did to Mr Vaughn. Please try to make sure that Mr Vaughn has my letter and give Mr Lanyon a message that I would like him to visit me as soon as possible.'

The last slipper was fitted and the dancing masters left, and Helen was delighted with her finished product, but Charmian gazed at her reflection with foreboding. 'I shall be stiff and nervous,' she said. 'There will be girls who have lived in London and not on a farming estate in Wales and a manor in

Somerset.'

'You will be the one they remember, although I hardly recognize my own lamb,' Debbie said with pride.

'I shall be forgotten easily. Even a friend who I thought was true has forgotten me,' she said sadly. 'You have no need to worry, Debbie. I shall not be swept off my feet by any of the effete young men I shall meet and I shall hate sitting in hot overcrowded rooms, smiling at people I don't know.'

Helen listened to her grumbles with patience, convinced that once Charmian had tasted popularity and attention she would enjoy life to the full. 'We must find you a companion,' she said. 'A girl of your own age with no fortune who will welcome your patronage.'

Mr Dark heard what she said. It might make Miss Charmian more contented. He left for Lincoln's Inn Fields for a few days, taking with him more messages for Mr Vaughn if he could reach him.

Charmian felt a stab of conscience that it was her fault that he had gone to Baden and not to Hornbeam Manor because she hadn't invited him formally. I do miss him, she thought and wandered into the library. It would be good to work there again but her new elegant shape didn't lend itself to reaching for books. She wondered if Helen would notice if she loosened her stays.

A letter arrived from Mr Lanyon saying that Mr Vaughn was not back yet but they would be coming later to the Manor together. Also would she receive a young lady who would be with them. 'She would be a suitable companion for you if you wish, my dear. One day Lady Altone will go away and you will need a companion. This lady is my brother's child, now an orphan of slender means, but I hope you will find her compatible.'

Charmian danced round her room, returning to her old gaiety until Pru told her to deport herself like a lady.

'But it will be so pleasant to have company again. Mr Vaughn is better. We shall *all* see him again and recall how kind he was in the past.' As an afterthought, she said, 'A companion might be acceptable too, if she is cheerful.'

Somehow the lessons seemed less arduous and Charmian awaited the arrival of her guests with impatience. They would come on the day she was presented. 'If they come early, they may see you in all your finery,

Lady Charmian,' Pru said. 'How surprised Mr Vaughn will be to see his little helper so transformed.'

'Do you think he'll notice?'

'Him and a hundred more,' Dermot said. 'Take care the gentlemen don't want to fight over you.' He stopped, aghast at what he'd said. 'I beg pardon, Lady Charmian. I didn't think.'

'There has been enough blood shed, Dermot.' She clenched her hands. 'In many ways I feel responsible for Mr Vaughn's wound and the duke's death. Their blood will be with me for ever, even though justice prevailed.'

'Mr Jaspern escaped,' Dermot said.

'He was weak and headstrong but young enough to make a new life, so what would be the use of hanging him? He is out of England now and we shall not see him again, so I hope he prospers.'

'You mustn't let your soft heart be hurt by such as he. You know now that a handsome face can hide a twisted soul.'

'Not all handsome faces hide wickedness,' she said wistfully, 'but I have no ambitions to fall in love or to indulge in dalliance at the assemblies. I may even return to Wales once I have been presented.'

Dermot smiled. 'I think you might find it dull there, after all this. Do not make any hasty plans.'

Sixteen

The first blossoms of May were opening when the shining carriage came to the door to collect the lady of Hornbeam Manor for her debut in Bath. The coachman and Dermot were dressed in new livery and the family crest glowed on the new blue velvet cushions and rugs. The sun shone and the late afternoon was warm, allowing Charmian to wear the lightest of wraps over the court gown. Kavanagh, the cat, curled up on a stone urn, watching, his slit eyes seeming to gleam approval. As the wooden steps were lowered for Charmian's dainty feet and Debbie fussed around her skirts, making sure they didn't crease, another carriage drew up on the other side of the driveway and a man and a woman alighted. Charmian brushed aside the caring hands and stared at the couple, her heart beating fast.

The girl was pretty and about her own age. That much she expected, but not as pretty as that, and she had no right to smile up at the handsome man at her side when he helped her from the carriage. This was no homely companion, a waif in the care of a crusty old lawyer. Mr Vaughn looked taller than she recalled, and broader in the shoulders, or was it because he was thinner? He was perhaps too thin, but even more good-looking than she had dreamed. He was dressed elegantly, as a gentleman of means, expensively attired but without undue ornament. He smiled at the girl and said something that made her laugh, then turned to Charmian and walked slowly towards her over the gravel, his face unsmiling, and Charmian offered her white, gloved hand. He stared as if he couldn't believe his eyes, then touched the glove with his lips and released it, backing formally away. 'Your servant, ma'am,' he said, in a low voice.

His hair seemed darker, his face thinner and his eyes had known pain. All this flashed through her mind and she wanted to kiss away the stress and smooth the lines round his mouth, but she took refuge in the tinkling laugh so newly taught, to cover her confusion.

'La, sir, what a time to arrive! But you are welcome ... and your lady.' She sat erect, with the posy that she must carry when presented to the Prince, tight in her hand, like a princess on an ivory miniature, framed in blue velvet. The coachman drove on.

Helen sat on the other seat, her attention taken by her own skirts, and she failed to see that the girl was close to tears.

Jack Vaughn with a woman? It was true that Charmian expected her, but Mr Lanyon had said nothing of the pretty face and the ease with which she conversed with Mr Vaughn. The carriage swayed round the corner by the chestnut avenue where she had walked so often with Mr Vaughn, laughing and gathering shining horse chestnuts. She glanced up through the canopy of light green leaves and the closely packed buds that would soon burst into a cloud of sighing white candles. It was spring, the time when all things grew and when every living thing was fresh and young and the sap was rising.

She couldn't rid her mind of the face she had just seen for the first time. A year ago, I was like that, she remembered. It was almost a year now since her father was killed and died under a sprinkling of creamy white roses, a year in which much had happened to bring sorrow, excitement and happiness. Jack Vaughn had smiled at the girl with the same good humour and tenderness that he'd once kept for Charmian Altone.

'La, child, you will ruin your posy. Have a care and give it to me. Place your hands in your lap until we reach Bath.' Helen smiled. 'I know that this is the most exciting day of your life but you are a lady and ladies do not show emotion in public at this stage.' It was a lesson that Charmian had learned well and she took a deep breath and sat tall. 'When we arrive, you haven't forgotten what to do?' Charmian managed a smile but as the carriage swung through the villages and over the river and she saw the noble lines of Bath Abbey, she wished with all her heart that she had never set foot in Somerset, never met Helen and all the good and evil she had brought; and she wished she had never met Jack Vaughn, the man with the gentle strength, whose eyes had forgotten to smile at her.

Bath was in a state of fête and festival, with bright ribbons and flowers in the streets. The roads were newly swept and shops full of expensive fripperies coaxing money from visitors who lined the Abbey Square to watch the Regent and the gentry arrive. Red carpets were positioned wherever the Prince was likely to walk from the Abbey to the Assembly Rooms and the Roman baths. It was rumoured that he'd planned a reception with his guests all dressed in Roman togas and the ladies in flowing white robes.

Helen referred to the programme they would have to fulfill and she seemed like a creature released from bondage, bowing gracefully to the crowds and enjoying being in the public eye again. They walked past the crowds that applauded each beautiful woman as she went into the Rooms, escorted to the main salon. The long wait began, with debutantes looking covertly at the other dresses, to see which gowns were richer than their own. Helen was complacent. 'There isn't a gown or a jewel to match yours, my dear.'

It was impossible not to be touched in spite of her sombre thoughts and Charmian began to enjoy the novel experience of being on view before so many. 'You look as elegant as any here, Helen, and much more beautiful,' she said generously, for since Helen had resigned herself to a subordinate position and had no demands made by an extravagant and violent brother, she had become softer and her looks, although mature, were striking and her grace and sense of what was *comme il faut* made her a worthy duenna. She accepted that this was far better than languishing in a draughty and boring dower house in Wales.

The Prince arrived with his retinue, a glittering throng that made Charmian catch her breath to see the jewels, bright clothes and elaborate wigs. Against the grey silk wall hangings, it was as if an artist had painted a mural of beautiful creatures from legend. Charmian held her posy and adopted the required expression of near boredom, but her heart beat faster.

Helen led her to her sponsor, an elderly gentleman who had been a family friend of the Altones for years. He was soberly dressed but his buttons were fine emeralds set in gold and his lace the best obtainable from Brussels. He looked at Charmian with approval, and said to Helen, 'You did well by her, ma'am,' and Helen fluttered her eyelids and wondered if her days in society were perhaps not over.

Charmian ignored the long skirt and train held by a page boy in blue velvet and made her curtsey with grace and dignity. The

Prince held her hand for longer than was necessary and murmured an enquiry of Lord Saxom, her sponsor. As they moved on, many eyes showed interest and it was rumoured that the Prince had been impressed.

Young men lounged by the crimson crush bar, eyeing the debutantes as if they were assessing race horses, and Charmian walked past with eyes downcast, unable to use the coquettish smiles taught her. They were handsome and dressed with all the skill and finesse that fashion demanded, and some had pleasant and well-bred faces, but she saw only one face, a face that no longer smiled at her; a man who had found a girl fitting to his station in life.

After wine and refreshments, Charmian retired to rented rooms where Debbie dressed her for the evening soirée. Charmian allowed herself to be undressed, dressed, perfumed and powdered and bewigged as if she was a doll.

'Is my lamb tired?' Debbie asked.

Charmian smiled faintly. 'It is the excitement,' she said.

Debbie prattled on happily. 'Did you see the young men talking about you, Lady Charmian? This is a day you will remember all your life. It's true what Dermot said, that you'll be the toast of Bath. I can hardly believe that the baby I nursed on my lap...' She bustled about the room and the words flowed over the girl as if it had nothing to do with her. This was an exquisite strange creature being adorned, a girl with whom she had nothing in common.

She thought of the cool chestnut trees and wondered if Mr Dark would remember to exercise her favourite horse. Perhaps it had been done, with Mr Vaughn riding with the fresh-faced girl who needed no wig or beauty patch to make Mr Vaughn smile at her.

Charmian was swept into the evening's entertainment and her spirits revived with the dancing. She made play with her feathered fan and smiled at the wit of the men. She drank wine and ate delicate pastries and Helen, who was delighted with her, turned away to greet friends of her own. The fact that she had never appeared in public with Shalfleet and the fact that her brother had killed him in an honourable duel, made people convinced that he had been protecting his sister's honour. Helen found herself welcomed as a woman of taste and suffering. She was not slow to take advantage of the fact and acted accordingly.

Dawn was breaking when Charmian climbed into the carriage. Helen yawned on the other seat and they drove back home in silence, each with her own thoughts and weary to the bone. The chestnut trees were covered with light mist and the rising sun glowed pearly pink below the hills. Kavanagh stalked a bird which flew scolding, making the horses snort softly as Dermot and the coachman unharnessed them. The two ladies walked up the stairs of the silent house and Debbie, who had followed in another carriage with the sewing maid, prepared tisanes of camomile and lemon and poured water into wide bowls for washing. She helped Charmian to bed and the girl sank into a deep sleep, her head full of colour and sound, fine dresses and flattering remarks. It was a weariness such as she had never known.

As she sank into sleep, she recalled that tomorrow – or was it today? – she must attend a supper after a concert, the day after, ride with Lord Saxom and the young Marquis of Sunderland who had been so attentive last night. There was a full programme, enough to turn the head of anyone. She groaned and wondered if her head

271

would clear, her feet be less sore and her willpower strong enough to endure it all.

It was noon before Debbie drew back the window drapes and brought hot chocolate and *langes de chats* biscuits. Charmian stretched and blinked, and Kavanagh slinked in after the servant left the tray. He sat on the end of the bed, washing his face as if to shame her for her laziness. Charmian smoothed the soft fur and listened to his growl of contentment. 'If I could choose, I would stay in bed for a while, have dinner at four and come back to bed,' she said.

She giggled. What would Helen say? For her, the social scene was life blood and that ball had been of utmost importance. Charmian stirred when Debbie grumbled that the bath water in the hip bath was getting cold and Charmian bathed and relaxed. There was no need to smile or posture and Debbie soothed her as she brushed her hair. She dressed in a loose gown and soft pumps in spite of Debbie insisting that there might be visitors. 'Let Lady Altone entertain them,' she said firmly. 'I am far too weary.'

'After only one day? Come my lamb. This will not do. Are you not well?' Debbie touched her brow but found it cool. She brought a face mask of oatmeal and honey that Helen had prescribed, but Charmian turned away. 'But Lady Altone said—'

'I don't care! I hate it. I shall have enough rubbish on my face tonight. Oh, Debbie, need I go? Can I stay in my room and have a headache?'

'Lady Altone says that you are to wear the lilac and cream with the pearls,' Debbie said firmly. 'The Prince will be at the concert and you must look your best. Come my lamb, you know you like that dress and with fresh freesias from the garden and the pearls, you look lovely. The dress calls for roses but it is too early for them and violets wilt under the candles.'

Charmian looked out of the window down the avenue towards the hills. She saw three figures riding fast, the wind taking the men's coat-tails and the long scarf worn by the woman riding side-saddle with as much confidence as Charmian.

She heard laughter such as she had enjoyed when riding with Mr Dark or Mr Vaughn, and even with Melville in the scented autumn. It was spring now and everything was growing or getting restless. Even Kavanagh stayed out at night, yowling for a mate, and all young men and women turned to thoughts of love. Was not this a time for wooing?

The figures now were easily visible. Mr Dark came a bad third in the race but all were laughing as they turned under the archway leading to the mews. It was as if a barrier came down between the lady of the manor and her friends in a way that showed how different their lives would be in the future and how little contact she would have with them.

Helen glided in, dressed in a soft afternoon gown, more dignified than the ones she wore with Shalfleet. She eyed Charmian's smock with distaste and Debbie shrugged as if it was none of her doing.

'Invitations are pouring in,' Helen said with satisfaction. 'Several messengers in full livery have already called, with billets doux from some of the most important families. I am proud of you, my dear.'

'I owe it all to you, Helen,' Charmian said politely and Helen was too absorbed in her plans to see the quizzical expression in the girl's eyes and the sigh she gave as she went to change into something more suitable.

A welcome break came at last when the Prince was summoned to London on matters of state and Charmian turned her back on the giddy whirl of dances, concerts and eager young men. The endless titbits she had to eat in every house she visited had become boring and she wanted plain food. Helen organized an exclusive dinner party at Hornbeam Manor, after which many guests came for dancing and left after three in the morning leaving the scent of violets and French perfume long afterwards.

Charmian sent for Mr Dark during a brief moment alone that week and asked if Mr Vaughn would come to the dinner as he had eaten with the family when he was living there.

'I am sorry, Miss Charmian, but he left three days after he brought Miss Lanyon here. I know he will be disappointed but he had to leave on business.'

'His business or mine?'

'A little of each, I think. I am unsure when he will return but he may be here after the concert at Keynsham Park.'

Charmian tossed her head. 'I haven't set eyes on him since he arrived and now he goes away just when I have time to see him,' she said in a vexed tone. 'I feel no guilt that he was neglected as I saw him riding with you and Miss Lanyon. Lady Altone told me that you entertained each other well.'

275

Mr Dark smiled. 'Miss Lanyon is charming and has won all our hearts.'

'Then if Mr Vaughn is not here I will see Miss Lanyon. I have not had time to see her properly and I have yet to decide if she is suitable for me as a companion.'

Mr Dark flushed deeply. 'Miss Lanyon also is away, Lady Charmian. She returns tomorrow night. She stayed for three days and did not gain an interview with you, so she asked if she might visit relatives in the district. I am sure that you will find her an amiable companion.' His anxiety was marked.

'We shall see,' said Charmian coldly. 'I saw only a glimpse of her and I must wait until I meet her before I decide what to do about her. She might be better employed looking after the young children of my cousin in Wales. For Mr Lanyon's sake I must see her settled.'

She turned away and Mr Dark felt dismissed. So, she thought, Mr Vaughn was not ready to wait patiently for her to see him, and to cap it all, that smiling little minx has bewitched him and is not here when required. She pulled on the bell rope so fiercely that it broke. Had they gone away together? Would they come back simpering and ask for her blessing on their betrothal or even return wed?

She was in a bad mood at the concert but at least she knew now why she had seen nothing of Mr Vaughn or the girl who hoped to be her companion. They could both go to Wales and she need see neither of them again. She heard little of the music and her smiling mask hid a deep loneliness. Even Mr Lanyon had gone away after a day and Mr Dark was the only intelligent company she would have.

After the concert, Charmian went back to Hornbeam Manor and sent the carriage back to wait for Helen who was having a very enjoyable time with a family who wanted her to groom their daughters for their coming out. She had hinted that she might have to leave Charmian soon and was very pleased with the terms offered for her expertise. It was good to know that Helen would make her home elsewhere but if she went, Charmian would be really alone, and she had come to respect the woman who had so nearly ruined her life with her efforts to make her marry Melville.

If only Mr Vaughn wasn't involved with Miss Lanyon. Charmian tried to be honest. The girl had good looks and a sense of humour and would make someone an excellent companion. It would be good to have a girl with whom she could giggle and share mutual interests but having seen her with Mr Vaughn, that was out of the question. If they were together under her roof, she would have nothing left but a memory of a strong shoulder and the scent of roses in the moonlight.

She undressed and sent Debbie to bed. 'Stay there late tomorrow,' she ordered. 'You have worked too hard and you are exhausted. I shall take chocolate in my room and perhaps ride before I interview Miss Lanyon.' She felt safe from meeting Mr Vaughn or the girl if she rose early.

She was up early, awakened by bird song and the rustle of silk by the four-poster bed as the breeze caught it. Kavanagh sat by the open window, washing cream from his whiskers. Charmian rang for a maid and sent her to ask Mr Dark to be ready to ride as soon as possible. It would be like old times, she told herself, and went out to see the groom as he led her horse to the mounting block. It was her new grey and she admired the fine head and restless eyes. 'You'll need to keep a tight rein, My Lady. He needs working and has had only a run with the stable lad for the past few mornings.' He grinned. 'But he's a beauty, ma'am. Let him get blown a bit before you let him go.'

'This gives me great pleasure,' Mr Dark said when he greeted her. 'And when you meet Miss Lanyon, you will receive even more pleasure,' he said. 'When you see how amiable she is you will like her.'

'Enough of that until after our ride, Mr Dark,' she said, her smile suddenly clouded. 'I must blow away the cobwebs of Bath and the heat and smell of wax candles.'

She walked the horse and gentled him, aware of his freshness. The sun made dappled shadows on her green velvet habit and the glossy hair flowed deeply auburn under her sweeping hat. The stock at her throat made her look at once boyish and intensely feminine, lacking the contrived elegance of the past week and giving back the appeal of youth and complete health. They rode together, the soft grass bruising under the fast hooves. The air was clean and a new happiness lingered on the edge of her earlier depression, as yet unsure if it had a place in her mood.

Mr Dark rode in near silence, sensing her mood. They picked late primroses in the copse and turned back. The grey was still lively but Charmian had taken all the exercise she could bear from him as she had to work all the time, conscious that he needed less oats and more brisk gallops, and her arms ached with concentration as she was afraid to let her control slip.

'I want to go back,' she said. 'I am tired and enervated by all the rich food and lack of exercise. We both need more rides.'

The gravel crunched and they were back in the avenue. Charmian's heart seemed to contract in an iron band. Mr Vaughn and Miss Lanyon were standing by the house, deep in conversation. Hearing the horses, they looked up. Mr Dark rode towards them round the central flower bed but Charmian perversely went the other way, avoiding the couple and making for the gateway to the stables. She saw the faces of the man and woman, staring at her, and she managed a smile, suddenly shy. It was so stupid, but the rift between her and Mr Vaughn was deep. Could it ever be bridged now to let them return to the simple pleasure and under-standing they had shared? She longed to jump down from the saddle and greet him as the friend he surely still must be, and to make the smiling girl welcome, but she urged the horse on, ignoring the groom who had come to take his bridle if she wished to dismount at the block by the front entrance. When he saw that she was riding to the stables, he ran back to be there when she needed him, and the welcoming smile died on Jack Vaughn's face.

Charmian bent her head, her eyes stinging with unshed tears and she did not see the small animal shoot out of the flower bed in pursuit of a bird, but the horse saw something small and fast and stopped abruptly, taking his rider by surprise as he reared up and turned. A cry came from the girl under the porch and an exclamation of horror from Jack Vaughn as he ran to take the bridle.

Too late to stop the horse from bolting, he caught Charmian as she fell, and clasped her, half-fainting, in his arms. She lay still, and as he had carried her after her father was killed, he once more carried her close to his breast. He placed her on the leather settle inside the library and knelt by her side, his concern overcoming the memory of her coldness.

She fluttered her eyelids and her colour returned. She looked up to see him gazing at her, his eyes filled with something so dazzling, so unexpected that she felt tears well up and threaten to overflow on to her cheeks.

'Jack,' she said in wonder. Could this be the man ensnared by Miss Lanyon? Could he look as he did now, if his heart belonged to another woman?

He took her hand and pressed it to his lips, his eyes now tightly shut as if to blot out the agony of seeing her fall. 'Charmian, my darling,' he said. The words were wrung out of him as if they caused him pain, as if they must be said, although he knew that his hopes were doomed. But it also held a question that was not being asked by a humble member of her household. His voice was that of a man who doubted if she loved him, but who had the right to ask her as an equal.

A movement from the doorway made her glance at the man who stood with one arm round the shoulders of a trembling girl. Mr Dark seemed completely at home with Miss Lanyon, as she rested her head on his shoulder as if that was where it evidently felt at home. They saw that were not needed and softly left the room, closing the door behind them, and Mr Dark told Debbie that Mr Vaughn wanted to talk to Miss Charmian in private.

Charmian smiled tenderly. It was all so clear now. Miss Lanyon was a thoroughly charming creature who would marry Mr Dark and live on the estate as a part of the life there. She found herself drawn into a close embrace and forgot everything she'd learned of coquetry. What did it matter if society scorned her for loving a man with no title? She would be happy again and go back to the hills of Wales. Her unbound hair was a shadow on his dark coat, his lips soft and reverent on hers as if she had performed an impossible miracle.

'Why did you stay away?' she asked.

'I had to leave this place until I could offer you the position that you deserve.'

'That is not important,' she said firmly. 'I want nothing but your love. I shall not return to Bath or to any of the stupid assemblies planned for me. Can we not go to Wales and let the world forget us?'

'No,' he said. 'You have a position to fulfill. There are many people who have worked hard to prepare you for this and it is what your father would have wanted.'

'They will take you away from me,' she whispered. 'I could not bear to lose you again.'

He kissed her with passion and her spirits soared to meet his own. He smiled, teasingly. 'It delights me to know you would want me even if I was but a humble secretary, but that is in the past. Mr Lanyon will be here directly to tell you all the dry details so I will not waste our time together, but let it suffice that he has traced a title that lapsed when it was thought there was no heir on my mother's side of the family. She came from Scottish–French stock and Mr Lanyon worked dilgently to prove that my claim is true. In Scottish law, a title can go through the female line and so it comes to me.'

'Go on,' she said, her eyes sparkling.

'I cannot speak to you until I have asked your guardian for permission, my love, but I want my wife to have been presented at court and to help me with the heavy burden of caring for the many estates in Scotland and my interests in Europe.'

Dermot tapped at the door. He was smiling. 'I beg pardon, sir, but can you receive a visitor, ma'am?'

'Who is it, Dermot? Lady Altone will receive today. I have every excuse as I was thrown from a horse!'

'This is not from Bath, ma'am. Mr Lanyon is waiting to see you and to renew his acquaintance with Lord Glencare.' He bowed low, his eyes twinkling with delight. He reached up to the weapons and trophies on the wall and took down a knife encrusted with jewels. It was short and slim and sheathed in rich leather. Lord Glencare took it from him, smiling. 'With your permission, ma'am, as it isn't my place to say, but I think that Lord Altone would want you to have it.'

'Why that knife?' asked Charmian.

'It is a skean dhu, the knife that Scottish noblemen wear with the kilt.'

Charmian laughed. It was all so confusing but she was coming back to life. It was the springtime of her love. Kavanagh sat regarding his mistress's happiness, by him a bowl of half-opened early roses, the rose called Moonlight, unfolding too into summer and bringing happiness.